THE HISTORY MAJOR

A Novella

MICHAEL PHILLIP CASH

ISBN: 1518893791
ISBN 13: 9781518893797

Praise for Michael's books:

Brood X: A Firsthand Account of the Great Cicada Invasion

"Horror at its best…up close and personal, and inflicted with ways that address humanity's inherent fear of and disgust for bugs."

—Mark McLaughlin, *Foreword Reviews*

The Hanging Tree: A Novella

"A short but mesmerizing tale, this spine tingling test of the human spirit quite literally takes on the ghosts of our ancestors in an attempt to neutralize their mistakes."

—Foreword Review

Stillwell: A Haunting on Long Island

"Cash makes the pain of a man who lost the love of his life palpable in this supernatural thriller with a genuinely surprising resolution."

—Publisher's Weekly

The Flip

"Cash's breezy prose and sharply drawn characters shine…he executes haunting scenes with a perfect balance of style and substance…a deliciously deft horror page-turner."

—Kirkus Reviews

The After House

"Cash delivers another emotionally rich haunted-house tale, filled with tantalizing history and Long Island color...the story is often quite funny...the supernatural and romantic elements seesaw back and forth nicely, and the historical scenes enliven both aspects...A charming, uplifting paranormal romance."
—Kirkus Reviews

The Battle for Darracia: Books I, II, and III

"This dynamic fantasy world is sure to entertain, as political intrigue, family turmoil, and vivid characters drive the plot forward...a fast-paced novel that will appeal to lovers of science fiction and fantasy. Set on an alien planet, this is a story about social equality and the struggles faced by those seeking great change...The author has crafted a complex society with a well-defined class system facing a political struggle for social equality. This is the first installment of a planned series, and Cash does a fine job laying the groundwork for future books. Schism is a quick, pleasurable read that is sure to entertain."
—Foreword Reviews

Witches Protection Program

"Badges and broomsticks collide in 'Witches Protection Program,' a fast-paced, lighthearted piece of crime fiction with a supernatural twist from screenwriter and novelist Michael Phillip Cash...With its lively characters, quickly moving plot, and amusing dialogue, 'Witches Protection Program' is a great summer choice, ideal for beach or poolside reading, and with elements of romance, action, crime, and fantasy, there's a little something for everyone to enjoy."

—Foreword Reviews

Pokergeist

"Cash proves to be highly capable of juxtaposing the absurd and the mundane, creating a thoroughly enjoyable ghost story along the lines of *The Canterville Ghost* (1891) and *Topper* (1926)… Bet on this funny, well-written tale of second chances."

—Kirkus Review

Pokergeist won the Grand Jury Prize in Comedy in the 2015 New York Screenwriting Contest!

Monsterland

"It is a dream team work for Young Adults and for those older adults to kick back and get with the current mania for themes of the undead. Another Cash in for Michael Phillip Cash!"

—Grady Harp, Vine Voice

For Ellen
(1951–2015)

Those who do not remember the past are condemned to repeat it.

—*George Santayana*

History is not a burden on the memory but an illumination of the soul.

—*Lord Acton*

Chapter 1

Amanda Greene lay facedown on the bed, her nose squashed against the scratchy blanket. She became aware of the smell first—musty, with the hint of sourness that comes from too much vodka on an empty stomach. She sniffed, rubbed her aching eyes, and then rolled up, the light sending darts of pain all the way to the middle of her fuzzy brain.

Groaning, she fell back and tried in vain to pull the thin cover over her gummy eyes. It was trapped beneath her body, but she continued to tug crankily.

"Shut the lights off, Danielle," she wailed, surprised that her voice was this thin, reedy thing. She tossed restlessly, something hard digging into her thigh. She shifted, causing it to dig deeper. *That's going to bruise*, she thought absently. Reaching beneath her leg, she pulled out her phone. Swiping her finger across the surface, she squinted. She propped herself onto her elbow and looked at the smudged face of her cell. Seventeen missed calls. She scrolled down; more than half were from her mother. *What does she want?* Amanda groaned, her head falling back heavily onto the mattress. They had only just reconnected, and now her newly divorced mother wouldn't leave her alone.

"Danielle," she said. "Kaitlyn?" She called for her two best friends. Her knee throbbed. She rubbed it absently, the skin raw and sensitive. Her rib cage screamed when she moved. *Ugh, what did I do to myself?* she wondered.

The phone vibrated impatiently in her hand. She looked at the illuminated screen, disappointment blooming in her sore chest when she recognized the number was not Patrick's. Her mother. Again. Really, her mother had virtually ignored her for four years after Amanda moved back with her dad. It had taken her mother's second divorce and the death of her beloved grandmother for them to reconnect at all. It hadn't been all peaches and cream, either. Just recently they had developed a wary sense of appropriate—unless there was a phone involved, apparently. Her mother never understood boundaries. Amanda threw her phone onto the floor, wincing when it made a crunchy sound.

Something fluttered from the corner of her eye. It changed the quality of the light in the room, playing with the shadows for a second. She raised her impossibly heavy head and looked through squinting eyes, but she couldn't quite see anything. Her head was loaded, as though it weighed too much. It fell back onto the tousled sheets. Movement by the window competed with her attention again, but she didn't have the strength to look at it. Her belly spasmed with anxiety, and inexplicably, her eyelids prickled as if she were going to cry. She stretched her right hand to the messy side table, searching for her antacids, but her fingers fumbled with her collection of pill containers, all of them empty. She cursed long and loud, throwing the amber-colored container against the wall with a loud crack. Patrick had said he would reorder her prescription. He always took care of her, reminding her to renew her megastrength stomach meds and antianxiety pills. *Yeah, well, that was before yesterday*, she thought angrily. Her bottom lip trembled, but she fought the feelings of hurt and despair with deep, painful breaths. She sucked in air through her nose and exhaled slowly through her mouth. It left her lightheaded, the gut-wrenching, twisting pain persisting.

She shuddered and rolled onto her back, a chill caressing her shoulders, the knowing feeling of something hovering just out of her line of sight. It was a rapid movement, both teasing and elusive. It had to be a bird. She lay sprawled on the bed motionless, watching the play of light against the white wall of her room. The shape altered, like a pulsing lava lamp. She dismissed the annoying outline. It waved again, persistently. She tried to calm herself, forcing the noise and light attacking her sensitive eyes and ears to close down. It was no use. Everything ached, and, for the third time, she tried to remember what had happened after they started drinking shots. She lay there, her arms thrown wide, her hands floppy and useless, her mind in a weird limbo, replaying her conversation with Patrick in her head.

Movement by the window competed with her wandering attention. This time it banged on the glass so hard that she recoiled, afraid the window would break. Blinking hard, she twisted, suspiciously watching the large pane of glass in the center of the wall. It remained whole, the silhouette gone. The quiet was so thick, it weighed her down. The light flickered. Amanda craned her neck, feeling a muscle cramp paralyzing her with pain. "Ouch," she cried out, angry at the world, but mostly at the specter taunting her vision peripherally.

Hitting the lumpy mattress, she pushed herself up. Her backside wobbled, and then she lost her balance as she grabbed uselessly at the blanket, sliding onto the hard floor with a loud thump.

She perused the vaguely familiar room, her mouth so dry it was actually painful.

She got clumsily to her knees and pulled herself onto the bed, closing her eyes against the bright glare from the drapeless window.

"You'll be late," an irritatingly cheerful voice warned. "Come on, lazybones. Time to get up. You have so much to learn."

Amanda put a flattened pillow over her head, shutting out the voice. Someone was pulling it.

"Manda," the voice sang. "You don't want to miss the first day! Isn't school fun!"

"Who are you?" Amanda's voice was muffled by the bedding. She rolled over, snatching the pillow to hold it protectively over her abdomen. She heard the familiar melody of a nursery rhyme, one of her least favorites, "The Muffin Man."

"Stop!" she snapped. She looked up groggily. Two faces swam before her. They wavered and then settled into a single image. Amanda studied the unfamiliar girl. "Do I know you?" Her voice was a rusty scrape.

The girl kept singing the irritating nursery rhyme. Her nasal contralto drifted into every nook and cranny of Amanda's abused head until Amanda's teeth drummed in time to the ditty. Amanda squeezed her eyes shut, holding her hands over her ears, the music growing louder until it sounded as though it were filling her brain.

She jumped up, bile rising from her stomach to bathe the back of her throat. She swayed, her eyes searching to find something solid to latch on to, to stop the movement. A wastebasket appeared under her face, and the booze from the night before made a horrifying return appearance. Kind hands held her long auburn hair from the mess while Amanda puked, and puked, and then puked some more.

Why did she drink so much? she thought bitterly. What was she trying to prove? Patrick's disappointed face swam before her eyes. She blinked hard, erasing his hurt hazel eyes and thinned lips. It wasn't her fault; it wasn't her fault at all. He had started the whole thing, forcing her to choose her friends over him. It didn't have to end up the way it did. She cursed softly.

A cold, wet rag efficiently made its way across her face, and the kind thoughts that were creeping their way toward her bitter mouth evaporated when Mary Sunshine piped, "Feeling better?"

Amanda took the washcloth from the capable hands, snarling, "Enough."

A beautiful face appeared before her weary eyes. "Too much?" the speaker asked, a sweet smile gracing her lips. She had a short pixie haircut, with feathery bangs framing ivory skin tinted with rose. Her large brown eyes observed Amanda sympathetically. She was tiny, her hands delicate, the fine bones of her face sculpted as if by a master. Impossibly long lashes swept her high cheekbones. Amanda wasn't overweight, but she felt oafish next to the girl's small frame.

Amanda cleared her gravelly throat. "What's your name?"

"You don't remember?" The girl pouted prettily. Amanda fought the urge to smack her. "I'm your roommate."

Did she have to sing every time she spoke? Amanda thought sourly.

"My roommate? I don't think so." Amanda glanced around the room. "What happened to Tonya?" Amanda got up, straightening her back. She heard a crack and winced as her knees creaked.

"Tonya? Who's Tonya?" Rebecca of Sunnybrook Farm questioned, her white teeth making Amanda squint from their brightness. She stared at Amanda as if Amanda were an idiot, her head cocked to one side.

Amanda gritted her teeth until they ached. The girl followed her as she paced the room.

"Stop that!" Amanda shouted, finding this stranger too close to her comfort zone. She could feel tiny puffs of air on her face and backed away warily.

She searched the tiny room. It was familiar. Two small twin beds were on either side of a blond wood desk. They were covered by cheap gray blankets and white linens. Where was her Trina Turk bedding, the turquoise-and-white trellis design she had picked out at Neiman Marcus with her stepmother? She walked over to touch the thin fabric of the worn blanket. She opened her mouth to say something.

"It's all here," the girl said defensively. Her eyes darted to a pair of desks squeezed into the tight room.

Amanda wobbled over to the furniture at the opposite wall. Two crappy-looking bureaus stood side by side; the only thing differentiating them was the surfaces. One was littered with all her things. She recognized the hot mess of her daily routine scattered across the top. A torn bag of chips, its contents half out of the bag, scented the room with stale oil. Her boyfriend's peppermint Lifesavers were strewn haphazardly across the top. He threw them there yesterday. Patrick's picture, the photo curling from neglect. She picked it up, touching his handsome face, angry at him for putting her in that position yesterday.

"He's cute," the other girl trilled. "You should put the photo in a frame."

Amanda looked at his face possessively. He was broad shouldered and tall, with wavy blond hair, cerulean-blue eyes, and a strong chin that was more forthright than stubborn. He was three years older, an engineering major with a prospect for a great job in Manhattan when he graduated. He was ROTC, but strangely, she was okay with that. She never thought she'd be dating a guy in uniform, but she understood he needed the money. The military helped with his tuition, defraying the costs of his education. She had met him during spring break last year in Cancun and discovered they would be going to the same school. They clicked with the intensity of a hurricane, becoming inseparable. He drove weekly on four-hour commutes to visit her once they came home, until she graduated, and then they spent the summer backpacking in Greece. Her friends were adamant that she was settling too fast, that she had her whole college career ahead of her. It didn't matter; Patrick made her feel complete. That was until yesterday. She stroked his wide cheekbones. Holly Hobby was right—she should have put the photo in a frame, she thought regretfully. Some liquid had stained the surface, marring his perfect face. She should have done a lot of things differently, her angry brain hummed. That feeling of being watched returned, burning a hole in her back. Amanda spun unsteadily, searching the room. She wobbled toward the window, and the other girl interrupted her. "Don't go there," the girl warned.

"What?" Amanda asked, stepping toward the window despite the warning. She was not one to take orders easily. "Why?"

Pixie Girl blocked her route. "There's nothing there," she said in that singsong voice. She took Amanda's hand, steering her away to another part of the room.

"Stop that!" Amanda shook her off. "You are really beginning to irritate me."

The photo of Patrick fluttered to the floor, and both Amanda and her bizarro roommate reached out to pick it up at the same time. Amanda grabbed it first and placed it on her dresser. She glanced at the other bureau. The gleaming top was organized, the bottles of lotions in size order, books neatly stacked. She picked up a bottle and looked at the unfamiliar name, then back at the stranger in her room, her eyes suspicious. This was not what she remembered. Tonya was, well, like her. "Where's Tonya's stuff?"

The other girl ignored her, busy tucking in her sheet with military precision.

She stared at her bed, frowning, trying to remember if something had happened to the comforter. Had she ruined it? She looked up in question.

A large green-and-orange school pennant spread across the wall over the roommate's bed caught her eye. She remembered it. "That was Tonya's," she murmured. She remembered thinking it was an odd choice for a cool girl, but who knew what was in anybody's mind? Giant posters of Nicki Minaj's shiny pink hair competed for space next to Drake and the Weekend over her own messy bed. Pasted dog-eared tickets surrounded Miley Cyrus's face—not the Disney one, the newer one, her tongue sticking out, her eyes maniacal.

Amanda glanced out the window, wondering why the girl wouldn't let her near it. The sun glared through the smeared glass, filling the room with harsh light. She was on campus. It was apparently morning, and, according to Tinker Bell, she was going to be late.

She glared at the concerned face studying her. "Tonya?" she tried.

Tinkling laughter filled the room. Amanda closed her eyes. When she opened them, she was alone. She spun, feeling her chest tighten with anxiety, but forced herself to breathe deeply to calm her nerves again. The roommate was gone. Her eyes scanned the room, looking at every detail, but the other girl had vanished. Maybe she had imagined her, and Tonya would reappear later. Amanda sat on the edge of the bed, counting out the facts she was sure of on her fingers. Number one, it was the first week of school. Two, she was in her dorm room, the one she had moved into a couple of weeks ago. Three, the bubble of her sweater squeezed into the shoddy dresser, preventing the drawer from closing the whole way, was just the way she had left it the night before, when she was here with Patrick. She remembered stuffing it into the tight confines of the drawer while he waited by the door. She knew she was where she was supposed to be. She shrugged. The pain had eased, only the dull ache where her heart beat wearily reminding her of her disappointments.

She walked slowly to the window and rested her hands on the filthy sill, her face pressed against the glass. It was so familiar, yet it had a strangeness, as if she'd never seen it before. It was different. Amanda let her eyes roam over the vista before her, trying to put her finger on the change. It seemed like yesterday that the landscape had been filled with lush, verdant leaves. The Indian summer refused to move on, the maples, hickories, and birches filling branches abundantly in varied shades of restful green, so that the school looked crisp, fresh, and inviting. Overnight, autumn painted a new picture, fading the landscape, ushering in the next season; the leaves withering, curling, setting the branches on fire with vivid oranges, yellows, and reds; the bases covered with the remains of dead leaves, shriveled and brown. It was too early; Amanda was puzzled by the change. A dark shape raced across the lawn, too fast for her to discern, but the feeling of unease returned. The shadow disappeared quickly behind one of the great gnarled tree trunks that Patrick had told her were the entrances for the goblins that terrorized the campus. She smiled, wishing Patrick were there so she could point it out to him. She squinted hard, trying to figure out what exactly had caught her attention, but the bleak landscape offered nothing. She laughed for the first time, her ribs protesting, missing Patrick so hard that it hurt more than her bones.

Amanda's brow furrowed, and the hammer clanging behind her eyes filled her skull, but the memory of how she had gotten there eluded her.

CHAPTER 2

Amanda stepped out of the shower, her bag of toiletries in her hand. Her head ached less, and her stomach gurgled noisily, letting her know her body was starting to work again. She looked at her reflection in the mirror. Two bloodshot blue eyes stared back stonily. Pale cheeks. Her hair was starting to grow in where she had shaved half her head a la Demi Lovato. She searched her trim thighs for the telltale cellulite that had started to dimple the smooth flesh. Too much alcohol, her stepmom had warned, but what the hell, she was just starting school. She had plenty of time to take off the freshman fifteen. She turned sideways, admiring the gentle slope of her back. Voices echoed in the tiled room, and Amanda briskly dried herself and slid into the new white robe her mother had sent for her to take to school as a peace offering. They had started talking recently, but Amanda found it hard to look her in the face. Her grandmother's death had opened the door for dialogue, but it was still hard. Some things were better left in the past. Padding to her room, she passed a hallway with doors on either side. Some were closed. Others were half-open. She paused, looking into identical rooms. Students were sitting or lying on their beds, studying or listening to music, playing video games. She nodded to the occasional wave of a hand. They all seemed familiar. Had she met them at orientation? She couldn't seem to remember. Patrick would know them. Names skittered in her brain but didn't stay there. Still lethargic from last night, she couldn't gather up any feelings to care.

Her room was empty, her roommate still gone. A piece of paper lay on her bed. It was a printout. Amanda picked it up, realizing it was her schedule. According to the timeline, she was indeed late for history.

"Huh," she said. She hadn't signed up for history. She loathed that subject, deliberately leaving it for next semester.

Amanda dressed and grabbed her bag, pausing by her dresser to stuff a handful of Lifesavers into her pocket. She hadn't eaten anything, and her mouth watered. She considered the last mint on the dresser and squeezed it from the cellophane into her mouth. The mint burst on her taste buds, bringing tears to her eyes. She missed Patrick. She wanted to call or text him. They needed to talk. She glanced around, looking for her phone, but it was gone. Shrugging, she hurried out the door.

The campus was bathed in soft light. Students walked in pairs briskly from building to building. Amanda stood trying to get her bearings. She paused and took in the riot of color painting the trees. It was all over the campus. *How could it have changed so quickly?* she wondered.

Something was wrong. Her eyes rested on the autumn landscape. Yesterday, it had been green, the warm air making it feel like May rather than September. Yeah, well, yesterday, she still had a boyfriend, she thought bitterly. A jet stream of cool air enveloped her, making Amanda wish she had taken a jacket. *When did this happen?* She looked around, unsure of her direction, her breath exhaling at the faded beauty of the surrounding landscape. It was as though she were in a bowl, a cornucopia, rich with the cinnamon and nutmeg fragrances she associated with Thanksgiving. The university was built on the estate of an old shipping family. The main building, the jewel of the campus, was a mansion, complete with a green-tinted copper cupola over its main entrance. The library was to the far left, easily recognizable by the Corinthian columns holding up the portico. The school stretched out before her, the rolling green hills dotted with a mixture of modern and Victorian buildings, a composite of old and new additions to the vast estate.

Her skin prickled again; she felt the sensation of being watched. Amanda turned around and walked backward, looking across the vast estate for the intrusive eyes. The wind ruffled the leaves. Amanda paused, searching for the discordant thing that pulled at her, but there was nothing out of place. She searched but couldn't find the cause of her uneasiness.

Huge shrubs waved gracefully, blocking the horizon. Many trees were splotched in oranges, yellows, and burnt umber, the colors blending where the branches met. A squirrel raced in front of her over the cobbled path, an acorn in its distended mouth. Amanda jumped back, startled by the rodent. A light breeze tickled her, blowing the curled brown leaves into piles that begged a dive. Amanda paused under a giant maple, the waxy red fronds dipping low as if to embrace her. She shuffled her clogged foot into a small hill of crispy leaves. Her heart felt like a lead weight in her chest. She looked at the library, missing Patrick. They had met there late yesterday to explore, then joined her friends at the campus bar. Was it only twenty-four hours ago that he had chased her up the gray-veined marble steps into the hallowed halls, their footsteps tapping on the tiled floors, their laughter earning them a stern warning from the librarian?

Sounds bounced around her, distorted, as if coming from a distance. Short bursts of buzzes and beeps that turned oddly longer, louder, until they faded. She spun and noticed the crowd had disappeared. The silence thickened; a giggle floated on the crisp air. Cocking her head, she held her breath, listening for the sound. The soft giggle reverberated behind her. She pivoted; losing her balance, she reached out for the hard bark of the maple to steady herself. It sparked beneath her hand, and she withdrew her fingers quickly, bringing them to her lips, blowing on the tender skin. She examined them and saw nothing but her unscathed hand.

Now the sound came from her left. She turned, feeling the utter absence of people, her breath quickening. Amanda nervously scanned the vista, feeling vulnerable, missing Patrick's strong presence. The wind ruffled the leaves, scattering them in an arrow shape. Wind chimes filled the air, and the laughter started again. Amanda's eyes opened with shock, and she gasped. She recognized the child's voice. She knew that voice, had heard it echoing in her own head. It was her own. She moved forward, her hands grasping her laptop tightly against her chest, as if it were a shield. She heard another voice, an older one, call, "Amanda…" She made a three-hundred-degree spin that both dizzied and disoriented her. Off balance, she dug into the rough surface of the tree, feeling a sizzle but holding on. The campus faded.

"Amanda…Amanda…" It was her grandmother calling her.

Amanda saw a child. She was no older than four, dressed in a jacket, her hat on the ground. The little girl ran behind the tree, her wide smile revealing a tiny dimple in her right cheek. She peeked from behind the trunk, her eyes mischievous. Her head was a riot of reddish-gold curls that framed the piquant face.

"Are you lost?" the little voice piped.

Amanda glanced around, looking to see whom she was talking to.

The girl inched out. "Are you lost?" she inquired.

Amanda pointed to herself. "Are you talking to me?" She moved closer, reaching out to touch the girl.

The girl backed away, a teasing glint in her eyes, and she laughed. "I don't see anyone else."

Amanda scanned the surroundings. "Lost?"

"Yes," the girl said gravely. "I think you are."

"I don't know what you are talking about." Amanda's mouth opened, her thoughts scattering like the leaves blowing down the path. She heard her grandmother's voice then, the warm velvet timbre that chased the demons away when she was little and ready for bed. The familiar nursery rhyme filled her ears, bringing tears to her eyes: "Have a taste of sparkly star, and drink a sip of moon, and when you feel as though you have gone far, then sail into your room."

"Nana," she whispered, her tear-washed eyes scanning the desolate scenery.

"Oh, I think you do know what I am talking about. When was the last time you were happy, Amanda? Do you remember?" The child turned, as if her name had been called, and with a joyous shout, she ran down a curved lane and disappeared around a bend.

"Happy?" Amanda whispered, watching the child run around the twisted path. Her grandmother's voice became harder to hear. She strained her ears, but it dissipated along with the clouds overhead.

Amanda looked down, noticing a crumpled woolen cap abandoned on the ground. She bent to pick it up and brought the soft mohair to her cheek. It smelled of apples and the wind. Dishes clinked, conversation rumbled, horns honked, and she could swear she heard the sounds of her favorite television show in the background. Taking a deep breath, she smelled pudding, rice pudding, filled with plump raisins. Her grandmother made it every time she visited. Memories rushed at her like a roaring tide. Her mint had disappeared. Her belly grumbled, her mouth watered, and the milky comfort of that thick dessert filled her heart with longing. Closing her eyes, she saw Papa Joe sitting in the old patched chair, the smell of cherry tobacco perfuming the air. She heard his wet cough and his gravelly voice calling for her to sit and watch wrestling with him. Hulk Hogan was going to be on. She pressed the yarn against her face, her breath hitching as if she had realized she'd lost something and suddenly found it. She jerked with a start, realizing it was hers, lovingly made by her grandmother. Her face crumbled, tears prickling behind her eyelids. She missed her grandmother, dead three years ago. They were close, even when her grandparents were forced to move to a warm climate for health reasons, until time and her grandmother's bad heart took her from Amanda's life. The wind whistled, whipping her hair against her stinging cheeks. She heard the child's giggle again, the knit cap curled in her fist. The voices faded. Amanda blinked, her eyes tearing. When she looked down at her hand, all she held were crushed brown leaves.

CHAPTER 3

The registrar's office was in the former stables. In the vee of a slight hill, the long building was white clapboard with forest-green shutters framing ten windows. Amanda opened the door to an overly warm room filled with a row of desks and a group of middle-aged women busy working. It sounded like a henhouse, the steady drum of their fingers mixing with cackles of laughter.

She approached the first desk, where a dark-haired woman was typing at her keyboard, her hair frozen in an upswept parody of a wave, her half-moon glasses perched on the end of her red-veined nose. A brass-and-wooden plaque identified the person at the desk as Beatrice Knockworthy. Amanda stared at the name, a giggle bubbling up. Ms. Knockworthy looked up, her mouth lazily chewing a wad of gum, her face an unwelcoming scowl, her ice-blue eyes assessing Amanda coldly. "Yes?" she inquired, her voice laced with suspicion.

"Excuse me." Amanda held out her rumpled paper. "It says here I have history," Amanda said impatiently. "I never took history."

The clatter of multiple sets of fingers hitting their keyboards stopped. Beatrice Knockworthy glanced at her fellow secretaries, a sly smile on her doughy face. Without another word, she grabbed the paper, her red nails resembling bloody talons. She looked up, her eyes assessing Amanda. "No, dearie, history is where they want you." She placed the schedule back on the counter.

She dismissed the girl, going back to her keyboard.

"I don't want it," Amanda said loudly. The room went silent.

"What?" Beatrice asked without looking up.

"I didn't take this class."

Sighing dramatically, Beatrice snatched the paper, then looked at the other women with a knowing nod. She typed in the information, the office workers watching with interest.

"Nope…" She handed back the paper. "History 101." This time the arctic eyes appraised Amanda up and down with a hint of interest.

Amanda looked at the paper, bringing it close to her face. It was barely legible, as if the printer was out of ink. "History 101, Professor…Totle." She squinted, struggling to read the lecturer's name. "I can't read this." She shoved it at the older woman. It fell onto the counter like a dead leaf.

"It won't matter." Beatrice Knockworthy took a file from a tall stack that wobbled dangerously and started typing, ignoring Amanda. Amanda watched the pile of manila folders sway precariously, amazed that nobody seemed to care.

Amanda realized the rest of these crazy women were staring at her, their mouths moving like a herd of cows in a pasture, all ten women chewing their gum with identical motions.

She stamped her foot with impotent rage, her hands fisted at her sides.

"You can take your attitude outside, Missy." Ms. Knockworthy dismissed her with a sniff. "You better take that thing and go." She nodded to the discarded paper.

"I don't want to take history," Amanda whined, picking up the schedule. "This was never on my schedule."

"Well, it is now."

"Remove it, then. I didn't plan for this."

Beatrice's face split into a widened smile, a great rumble of laughter erupting from her belly, which shook like a Jell-O mold. Soon, the office workers were all laughing together, great guffaws sending all of their oversized stomachs into a mass of wiggling, giggling shudders. Amanda watched in horrified fascination as they continued their absurd laughter.

The old woman wiped a tear from her eye, her mirth fading.

"I didn't," Amanda repeated after a long pause. "I don't like history."

"Well, dearie," Beatrice told her firmly, "*everyone* has to study history."

Amanda opened her mouth in astonishment. "Not me. I'm not going to go."

The older woman shook her head. "You don't have a choice. It says right here." She pointed to her monitor. Amanda leaned over the desk, trying to read the screen. From her position, it looked like a mess of numbers. A tapping at the window froze the conversation, and the women all turned nervously to their keyboards, their fingers working with maniacal speed, drowning out the sound of the rattling glass. It stopped as quickly as it had started.

A shadow darkened the window, casting a dark pall in the narrow room. Cool air surrounded them, and Amanda could see goose bumps cover their fat arms.

Amanda turned to stare at the window but saw nothing except the glare of the naked fall light.

Beatrice stopped what she was doing, her face going pale. She exchanged a look with the other secretaries. "You better get going."

"I need to speak with somebody with authority," Amanda told her with as much imperious dignity as her pounding head would allow.

Beatrice glanced at the window. The woman next to Amanda touched her shoulder, then shook her head, her voice a timorous whisper. "You have to leave. Now."

"Sorry. You better go. Class starts soon." A barrel-shaped woman stood on orthopedic-shod feet. She moved forward, her pudgy hands reaching out to poke Amanda. "Go!" she said urgently.

Amanda backed away, then stared at the creased paper in her hand, seeing nothing. "Is that all you are going to do?" She looked around the room.

"You better get going before…"

"Before what?" Amanda demanded.

"Before you miss the class." Beatrice dismissed her, spinning in her chair to type furiously at her keyboard. The women all resumed working with an indifference that rattled Amanda to her toes. She searched the room, looking for a door to a superior's office.

"Is there someone else who can help me?" she implored.

Beatrice held up a stick of gum, her face closing up. The subject was finished. "Gum?" she offered, her eyes narrowing.

Amanda crumbled the schedule in her fist and left the office.

CHAPTER 4

Amanda exited the office and searched the twisted path, seeing nothing but the sign for Hooker Auditorium. She glanced down at the paper, confirming that was where her class was located. Reluctantly, she walked toward the monolithic building. It loomed before her, blocking the scudding clouds that flew across the ice-blue sky. She stared at it, her eyes smarting. Angrily, she brushed away an errant tear and marched down the lane. The sun was high overhead now, taking the chill off the early morning air, yet Amanda's skin rippled as though a cold breeze blew.

The wind picked up, pushing her down the winding walkway to the large auditorium. She heard her name, grated out by a voice she didn't recognize. She paused, searching for the caller. Indecision warred, and she debated whether to return to the dorm rooms. She changed direction and began walking back, but a shiver of fear made her stop. She felt so alone. The campus was desolate. No birds flew in the sky; she didn't see a plane, for that matter, either. Amanda stood stock still, her eyes wandering the landscape, the invasive feeling of being watched filling her with a dread. It raked her skin, causing her to walk faster. She picked up speed, racing, the wind biting her cheeks, her hair whipping back. She felt a hard tug jerking her head. She sobbed loudly and dropped her things, feeling trapped. Frantically she twisted, her hair ripping from her scalp, caught on the crooked twigs of a low-hanging branch.

She laughed with an edge of hysteria coloring her voice, unbraided her hair, and then picked up her scattered belongings to rush headlong toward the lecture hall and the comfort of losing herself in the crowd surrounding it. Relief smothered her unease when she found the lane thickening with students. Undergrads milled about, holding laptops or books, casually talking in small groups. Amanda weaved through the crowd, searching for a familiar face. People largely ignored her. She sniffed, angry resentment settling in where nervousness had lodged. She was used to being with the popular crowd. Several of her high school friends were going to this school and had created an exclusive little group that included her. Sometimes they showed an insensitive side, but Amanda found it was both safer and easier to be with them than against them.

Snatches of conversations filled her ears, but try as she might, she couldn't make out a single word. She stopped and turned to look back at the registrar's office, but she couldn't locate it in the rolling hills. She scanned the horizon. The long, low building had apparently disappeared. It was probably in one of the larger dips in the hills, invisible from her vantage point. The feeling of unease settled in her bones, and again she wished she had her antacids.

Her feet dragged reluctantly, the crush of people propelling her onward. The group closed in around her, their smothering proximity pressing her toward the granite steps. Well, she would go today, she gave in ungraciously, and lodge a complaint later. She looked backward, wishing she knew what was causing the unsettled feeling, missing Patrick to chase it away. She wanted to call him, make him forgive her, but her phone was gone or broken, or whatever. She thought about what she would say to him, knowing she had to make it right between them. Being without him scared her more than the feeling of gloom that seemed to be chasing her.

Moving through the crowd, feeling secure once more, she planned another conversation in her head, a heated discussion with that Knockworthy person's boss. She would go above the secretary's head. With the tuition her dad was paying, the least they could do was listen. She searched the crowd again, her disquiet at not being able to find a familiar face making her feel small. A tiny knot of uncertainty lodged on her shoulder, weighing her down. The breeze whipped her hair, and her fingers threaded through the reddish locks to tame them.

She sucked in her breath abruptly, her skin crawling, apprehension that she was being watched making her skin crawl. Forcing herself to breathe deeply, she let her eyes search the rolling lawn of the campus, section by section. She worked patiently, as she remembered doing in one of those children's books when she tried to spot the person who didn't belong. No matter how slowly she scanned, it seemed to be ahead of her, just out of her line of sight, yet she couldn't shake the jittery feeling.

Amanda allowed the flow of the crowd to pull her up the eighteen stone steps into the vast auditorium. *There has to be seating for a thousand students*, she thought, amazed. She had chosen the school because it was a small college, one she wouldn't get lost in. That was the reason she gave everybody else. Really it was because it was where Danielle and Kaitlyn were going. The vast cavern seemed disproportionately large for such a small campus, as if it could fit the entire student body. She moved to one of the last rows, her face scrutinizing the crowd, her teeth worrying her bottom lip in the hope she'd find one of her friends. She inched slowly toward the least conspicuous seats, watching incredulously when they automatically filled, students pouring into the room like an incoming tide. Despite digging her feet in, she was pressed toward the front of the lecture hall, as if on a wave. She coasted to the second row, the surge of students lifting her so that she landed in the middle, settling directly before the lectern. Great. She winced.

No chance of dozing off now. Her face was planted right in front of the professor's spot. She plopped her laptop onto the wooden stand attached to her seat and opened it to find a program for notes. *Well, at least that's familiar,* she thought with a small degree of satisfaction.

The stage was dark, a single spotlight over the podium. There was a screen in the rear, its white surface reflecting the light so that it glared back at Amanda, hurting her sensitive eyes. The room was noisy with the shuffling of students, active conversations echoing off the walls. Amanda sank low, pushing her knees against the hard, bowed wood of the seat before her, shoulders hunched. The bruise on her knee reminded her of its presence, the ache in her side making her wish she had taken an aspirin. She peeked around, again hunting for a familiar face, grimacing when she failed to even elicit an answering smile from anybody. Lowering her eyes, she considered the students on either side of her. There was a light-haired girl, completely engaged in an animated conversation with the person on the other side. The girl gestured with her hands, her narrow back a cold wall preventing an introduction. The seat on the other side was occupied by a guy filled with all the brooding intensity of a gothic hero. He was so classically stoic. Amanda laughed, wishing Patrick were there so they could guess his major. *I bet it's political science or poetry,* she guessed, appraising him. He showed no interest in her. Amanda was not used to being ignored. She was pretty in a wholesome way, with round cheeks framed by waves of reddish hair. Her green eyes sparkled when they weren't bloodshot. Her pert nose, firm chin, and ready smile promised animated conversation. She had finely arched brows that rose across her high white forehead when she was amused. Amanda stole a look, raising those eyebrows with curiosity. She saw only his profile, but it was enough to tell her he had dark hair, olive skin, a strong jaw, and the faint beginnings of a meager beard. She considered him for a minute, comparing him to Patrick's blond good looks. He ignored her. He looked familiar. *Do I know him?*

Amanda bit a cuticle, her thoughts racing. Was he a friend of Patrick's? Had they met at orientation?

She knew he was watching her now, from the corner of his eye, his hands laced casually on his stomach. She shifted in her seat, dislodging her bag so that it fell on his feet. He sighed loudly and then leaned over impatiently and slapped it back on her lap. He looked her full in the face, and she gasped, slightly breathless. She did know him. What was his name? She wracked her brain. Where had she met him?

He studied her, his face devoid of expression, waiting, the silence thick between them. He nervously watched the stage, as if he were waiting for a cue. He appeared to struggle. His mouth opened and then closed, as if he didn't know what to say. Rolling his eyes, he made an impatient noise and said sarcastically, "Come here often?" He watched her intently for a reaction.

"What?" Amanda asked.

"That was my pickup line." He paused. "Not interested?" He shook his head. Shrugging indifferently, he continued. "Well, I tried."

"Tried what?" She looked around him to see whom he was talking to.

He appeared lost in thought. Then, after a long pause, he abruptly changed the conversation, as if he were uncomfortable with her. "I've heard the professor's a real creep."

Well, that came out of nowhere, she thought. She opened her mouth to respond and then shrugged, glancing at the other faces nervously. He had begun this conversation, so she intended to continue it. He appeared to be the only one around who seemed moderately interested in talking. He was a bit socially off, but it was nothing she could put her finger on. Maybe he was as jumpy as she was. She rotated her head, wishing Patrick were there, the longing for him coming back so strong that she felt the flush of shame at her behavior last night. Patrick was a great guy, and she had blown it. She'd be lucky if he ever talked to her again. Her lips turned downward, her cheeks burning. She wished she had someone to talk to about it. Her face rose, and she realized the stranger was watching her curiously. As if a weight had been lifted, he smiled ever so slightly, just enough to make the unease dissipate. She thought about responding, but an apprehensive shudder shook her.

What if someone told Patrick they had seen her talking to another guy? She looked at her fingers pensively. Technically, they weren't together anymore, right? They had had a fight. She had stormed off to drink with her friends. He hadn't taken her home. That meant it was over. Besides, she thought, bristling, talking to another guy wasn't dating, it was just talking.

"Who? Totle?" She straightened up, her feet falling onto the sticky floor; Patrick was tucked away until she could sort him out. She didn't feel up to reexamining her feelings for him right now.

"Totle?" He laughed. "Who told you that name? Not that it matters. Either way, he's tough. Been here forever. He's some kind of genius or something."

Amanda took a deep breath and fully examined the speaker. He was maybe a year or two older than she, with soft brown eyes, his crisp dark hair pulled away from the lean lines of his face into a ponytail. He had long sideburns that disappeared into an artful stubble gracing his chin. Patrick had hardly any facial hair. Sometimes he was like such a boy, she thought. She studied the stranger, the feeling of recognition again making her think, where had she seen him? Maybe he was famous, like an actor in commercials. She wanted to ask.

"Have we met?" she asked.

His eyes opened a fraction wider. The lids stalled and then drooped lazily. He looked around and responded with a shrug. "It's a small campus."

He was wearing a white tee and a heavy motorcycle jacket. His black jeans had a rip at the knee. He jiggled his leg nervously and turned back to the front of the hall, apparently finished with their conversation. He was the first moderately friendly face she'd seen since waking this morning. Truth be told, she thought, she was beginning to feel isolated, as if she were in a foreign land rather than her school. She expected a bit of disorientation; it's not every day that one starts college, but with her hangover, it was getting decidedly weird. She opened her mouth to draw him back into conversation, and the words froze on her lips. Her neck prickled. She stood and turned quickly to glance at the back of the hall. Her chest constricted, as if she couldn't draw air into her lungs. A sharp pain lanced her abdomen. Leaning on the back of her seat, she gripped the armrests, her knuckles whitening.

Twisting in her seat, she stared at the doors in the back of the auditorium.

She felt her companion abruptly stand, facing the back door, his feet planted wide apart, his face set.

She gasped when a black-gloved hand shook the handle of the glass door, pushing to enter. Amanda peered over the students' heads, frantically trying to make out the person struggling with the door. Her heart beat wildly in her chest. She couldn't explain the intense feeling of threat, but she knew he was there for her, and her alone.

The student next to her was as immobile as a rock, his strong presence calming her fraying nerves. The room grew quiet, and the intruder's hand paused. Fisted, it pounded the window so hard the glass rattled dangerously. A dark-clad shoulder pressed against the door, struggling to open it. Amanda dropped her things, feeling trapped. She pushed behind her neighbor, her body taut with anxiety, trying to move from the row. A steady hand gripped her forearm, the heat of his palm singeing her skin. She pulled away but heard his soft voice ordering, "Stay here."

His arms now folded across his chest, his eyes watching the door intently. His face was devoid of emotion, yet a nervous tic appeared in his lean cheeks. The air sucked from the room, Amanda struggled to breathe; a weight lay heavy on her chest. The fist pounded angrily, but the rest of the students were oblivious. Only the man next to her seemed aware of the threat. His jaw fixed, his eyes glaring, the student held out his hand, palm facing the door in the universal signal for *stop*. The rattling stopped, and the dark figure melted into the abyss beyond the hall.

Air rushed into Amanda's lungs with a rapidity that made her dizzy. She was pushed back into her seat. She looked up to gape at her new companion. "What just happened?"

"They're very strict here. They don't tolerate lateness."

She shook her head. "That wasn't about lateness. You made him leave. Who was that?"

"I did nothing." He sat down. "It was a latecomer, another student. That's all."

"No…I don't think so." Nothing was going right today. She turned her head to look behind them. The door was firmly closed; everybody was calmly settled in. Amanda shook her head. She felt…crazy. "I…It's just that…" She looked her neighbor straight in the face. What was she going to tell him? That she had had a sensation of being followed? That she had woken up after a night of partying and couldn't remember her roommate or her surroundings? Amanda bit her lip with indecision. Her reputation would be ruined before she even started class. College was all about new beginnings. Her grandmother had taught her to always forge ahead. Move through the challenges in one's path and push on. Forget the past. It had worked when she was a child—her grandmother's quiet strength had picked up her broken soul and made it whole when her mother had shattered her. Her grandmother had taught her to leave the past behind. History was history for a reason, and it wasn't the place to dwell. Her grandmother was right. When she wallowed in history, she was paralyzed emotionally. *Then what the hell was she doing in history now?* she wondered. Nobody knew what had happened to her when she was young. This was her fresh start. Some things were better left unsaid, she decided. Even thinking about it put her on shaky ground, made her world feel unsettled.

Taking a deep breath, she rallied and asked the student next to her, "Is this your first year here? Are you a freshman?"

"I've been here long enough," he said evasively.

"Okay." Amanda held out her hand, not quite sure what that meant. "Let's start over. I'm Amanda Greene."

There was an awkward moment of silence, and Amanda fought the urge to crawl under her seat. He seemed thoughtful.

She could swear his eyes looked shiny, as if he were almost… tearful. "Starting over." He rolled the words on his tongue, as if trying them out. "My name is Nick Fortune. Nice to meet you."

Amanda smiled with relief. "Yeah." She nodded. "Do you dorm here, or are you a local?"

Nick looked at her with a funny expression, and his head moved to the side. He was opening his mouth to answer when a great hush descended upon the room.

"Here he comes." He turned his attention to the stage, apparently finished with her and their conversation.

Amanda gaped at the man walking purposefully toward the podium. He was in his sixties, and a cap of thinning gray hair covered his head. He had a full beard that pillowed his chin, making him appear like the homeless people she saw on the news. More shocking than that, he wore a white toga, and leather sandals flapped against the hard surface of the stage. Gold bracelets adorned his forearms, and he wore heavy, chunky rings on each finger.

"You have got to be kidding me," she whispered, realizing that the professor had zeroed in on her face, his black eyes watching her intently.

"If this were a class on logic, I could spend the next ninety minutes discussing the reason for my appearance. It is explained extensively in my text *Organon*." He drew out the name slowly, his straight teeth showing brightly though his bearded smile.

There was the rumble of groans in the room. He held up a large square hand. "However, I have agreed." He wiggled bushy eyebrows to the group cheekily. "Under duress, but nevertheless, I have agreed to teach history this semester to you pack of beetle-witted, sorry excuses of humanity."

"Hey, we can't all be kings," someone shouted from behind Amanda.

The professor looked down on the students, his full lips pursed. "Quite so. True, you can't all be kings or conquerors. How boring for me." He sighed. "Alas, we must soldier on, inspiring notions in the dark, dank recesses of your unlit minds, sparking the fire of illumination." There was a collective chuckle. "So, instead, ladies and gentlemen, if you will open your texts to page four thousand eighty-five and discuss what you have read on the importance of dreams..."

"What...wait..." Amanda grabbed Nick's arm in panic, squeezing the spongy leather of his jacket. "Did I miss something? This is the first day...page four thousand eighty-two. I didn't..."

"It's four thousand eighty-five. Relax and listen. You'll catch on quickly. I did."

"Catch on!"

"Before the idea of sleep is fully examined, we must first realize that sleep occurs as a result of overusing one's senses," the professor droned on.

"Sleep?" Amanda repeated, her eyes wide. "I thought this was history," she whispered fiercely to Nick, who was busy typing notes.

"Don't make noise," Nick said harshly. "You'll piss him off."

"You again!" The professor pointed a long finger at her angrily. "If you had bothered to read my treatise on logic, you would understand the chain of thought! Care to share what you have learned these past few classes with your puerile friend, Mr. Fortune?" he demanded.

The room was deathly silent. Amanda shrank into her chair. Nick turned to her.

Wait, she thought frantically. *Past few classes? Where have I been? Did I miss something? Did I miss class?* Amanda's fisted hands forced small semicircular indentations from the pressure of her nails into the tender skin of her palms. Was this a dream? Her mind worked feverously, trying to piece things together. "What's today's date?" she demanded, her eyes wide with mounting horror.

Nick went on, ignoring her. "What I think our esteemed professor is trying to point out is that the chain of thought results in a systematic group of memories that create the laws of association. The professor believes"—he glanced up to the teacher as if for confirmation—"that past experiences are hidden within our minds." The older man nodded sagely. "He claims there is a force that awakens these memories. That power is association."

Amanda looked at Nick and then glanced uncertainly at the professor. It was like looking through a tunnel. Their voices came as if from a distance.

"Yes, Mr. Fortune. Logic, once again. First we have the experience, then the memory, which fades. We stimulate the brain with an image, and there you have it." He snapped his fingers. "The memory is activated by the…" He bent down, peering at Amanda expectantly.

Nick whispered from the side of his mouth helpfully, "Association."

"Association," Amanda repeated weakly.

"Yes," Nick said quietly. "Aristotle's theory on association."

"Aristotle?" Amanda exhaled the name. She looked from Nick to the educator on the stage and giggled. "Is this a joke, like where teachers dress like historical figures?" *Or a dream?*

"Silence!" the teacher's voice thundered. He stalked over to stand right before Amanda, his silver brows drawn together. The room was deathly silent. Amanda gulped so loudly, she swore she could hear it amplified in the room.

Nick held a finger to his lips. "Sh…" He nodded to the man on the stage.

The professor watched the exchange and said, "Babysitting, Mr. Fortune?"

Nick shrugged, and the nervous tic in his cheek appeared again. "Like I have a choice?" he said grimly.

"Where there is no guidance, a people falls, but in an abundance of counselors there is safety," the teacher intoned.

"Proverbs." Nick inclined his head. "Still, not what I expected."

"Some liken it to purgatory," the teacher said with a laugh. He glanced at Amanda's frozen face. "I'd rather have my fingernails extracted. We never tolerated these types of things in my day. Women…" He shuddered. "Are we quite finished?"

Nick glanced at Amanda, his face unreadable. He nodded, as if he'd accepted a responsibility. Amanda blinked, feeling like a silent observer to a private conversation.

"Excellent," the professor boomed. "Excellent. So we begin. Let us start with Joan of Arc…"

Joan of Arc, Amanda thought wildly. She didn't want to learn about Joan of Arc. She had read about her in religion class when she was seven. She hated history. She didn't need history. This was a waste of time. She stared at her laptop, her eyes filling. Turning, she looked longingly at the exit, lit up by a red sign. She half rose, tucking her computer under her arm. The click of her laptop closing caused the professor to stop his lecture and turn to her, his gaze searing.

"Are you, perhaps, going somewhere?"

Amanda shrank back into the seat, her face tight with shame.

She heard Nick's calm voice. "Just go with it. Close you eyes and picture what he's saying. It won't hurt a bit."

Amanda did close her eyes, but with humiliation. The professor cleared his throat noisily and then started talking again, his words washing over her. She relaxed back into the seat, her mind on her failed exit, the whereabouts of Patrick, the guy next to her, and the fact she was not going to enjoy this semester.

The teacher walked across the stage, his arms expansive, his voice melodious. The words made their way into the tight clamshell of her mind, taking root.

"Jeanne d'Arc, also known as the Maid of Orleans"—the professor used the French pronunciation—"was born around the year 1412 in northeastern France, in the scenic village of Domremy. Jeanne was the daughter of Jacques d'Arc, a farmer of about fifty acres. Jeanne was born into tumultuous times and began having visions when she was…"

CHAPTER 5

France, April 1425

*Children say that people are hanged sometimes for
speaking the truth.*

—*Joan of Arc*

The girl sat on her knees in the loamy soil. Fall had turned the
air sharp. She dug deep and pulled at the feathery tops of
the carrots. They remained tight in their earthen home, snug
and happy to stay there. She inhaled the freshness on her fingers, loving the fragrance of home, crisp vegetables ready to
be cooked by her mother. She was surrounded by plenty, from
the abundant kitchen garden that spread out for an acre on
the side of their home to the apples that hung in the orchard,
known far and wide for their juiciness. Squinting, she eyed

a lone apple swinging in the breeze, begging for an archery contest with her brothers. She pretended to hold a bow, carefully aiming and firing, celebrating when her phantom arrow hit its target. She chuckled at her marksmanship, then looked guiltily around for her papa. He didn't like it when she played at boys' games, but he never objected to the tender rabbits she brought home. At thirteen, she should be practicing to be a wife, not behaving like a wild child, and a boy at that. She shrugged, making a sound with her tongue, as if she cared about being a wife. She brushed her hands together briskly, shaking off the rich, dark soil. Still, she considered, she would have to organize a contest later, when her brothers returned from the wheat fields. It was too tempting to ignore. Jeanne sat back on her haunches, her long skirt pooling around her. A fat worm struggled on her flattened hem, trying vainly to return to his moist home.

"Juicy worm. You will make Pierre very happy when he fishes for our supper later." She picked up the slimy worm with her fingers, deposited it gently in her palm, and watched it squirm, its midsection turning purple from the effort. She tapped it gently on the head and then let her finger glide along its fragile surface. "Such an ugly little thing." She clicked her tongue. "Like me." Jeanne sighed. She was a plain little thing, she knew. Short and squat, with sturdy peasant legs, she was the despair of her poor *maman*. She held up one hand and looked at her work-roughened palm and indelicate fingers.

No matter how much she tried, she found no comfort at the spinning wheel. Her mother spent hours with both her and her sister, Catherine, showing them the ways of spinning so they could make the yarn that would clothe their own families when it came time to marry. Jeanne preferred to be outdoors, running with her three brothers, fishing, hunting, and rolling in the giant hay mountains at the end of the summer. It made Papa very mad, this side of her. She would never find a husband, he warned, if she didn't settle her boyish ways. She considered the worm wriggling in the cup of her hand. "You didn't choose to be picked for someone's dinner, my friend. Why should you be sacrificed for our pleasure?" She blew gently and watched the worm curl up indignantly. Jeanne laughed, her giggles floating on the afternoon air, the bobbing heads of flowers nodding in agreement. "I think *mon frère* will be very angry with me, but I haven't the heart to hurt you after such a deep conversation."

She rolled the worm into the clustered leaves of a fat cabbage, smiling as it inched away to hide. Jeanne lay back on one elbow, her apron wrapped around her hips. She reached up to remove the linen cap she wore, letting her dark-brown braid fall onto her shoulders. She flipped it out of the way. She hated her heavy hair, wished she could cut it off, like her brothers. It got in the way of everything. The thick, coarse braid pulled at her scalp, causing her more than a little headache. She played with the end, pulling at a split end, separating the strand so that it unfurled her tight plait, letting the brown cascade open like a fan on her back. The sun blinked, and the sky momentarily darkened. She shaded her eyes to peer at the strange change. She shivered as the temperature dipped, the dampness from the earth seeping through her skirt, making her whole body go cold. Above her, clouds rolled in, covering the entire horizon. She had never seen any formation like this before. Moving to her knees, she grabbed her cap and placed it on her head, knowing rain was imminent. She glanced worriedly at the clothes lying on bushes nearby, drying.

She rose to her haunches, ready to beat the rain, when thunder boomed so loudly the ground trembled. She turned frightened eyes to the sky. Jeanne's breath left her body. Crossing herself, she said a quick prayer, her lips moving automatically but the words spoken softly. The prayer slowed her rapid heartbeat, forcing her to calm. Still, her scalp tightened as the air changed, churning as if it were a raging current. The clouds were deep green and blue, with purple streaks looking like the deep end of the unfathomable lake at the end of the forest. Her skin prickled, goose bumps traveling up the fine muscles of her arms. She froze, gasping as the clouds moved and molded themselves as if a giant hand were shaping them.

Three figures slowly emerged from the clumps of clouds, shimmering brightly before her. The young girl scrambled to her knees, her hands shaking, both laundry and her escape forgotten, her hair a wild nimbus around her heart-shaped face. The world turned eerily quiet, and the dense clouds illuminated the sky, blocking any thought of escape, bathing both her tanned complexion and the land in a golden hue.

Wind whipped her face, tears ran from her eyes, and she looked away from a stunning brightness that lit the sky. Her thighs ached from her stance, and she dug her feet down, ready to run. A voice rang out, commanding her to stay where she was. Jeanne gripped the tiny silver cross she wore around her neck, holding it so tightly that it gouged her skin. "Sweet Jesus, protect me…" she repeated frantically.

Quaking with fear, she cowered until a gentle hand brushed the top of her head. Warmth surrounded her, like the security of her mother's touch, replacing her fear with a calmness that steadied her beating heart. Jeanne peeked up, her mouth open, her breath frozen in her constricted chest.

The figures were beautiful, all in silver and white, their skin luminescent as the finest pearls. There was a man, flanked by two females. They were so large they filled the sky. The man had an enormous sword at his hip. His glorious wings surrounded the women like a cape. They hovered above her, floating in the sky, bouncing as if they rode gentle waves. Their arms reached out to her. A fine golden ring circled each of their heads, pulsing with a life of its own, mesmerizing Jeanne.

"Are you an angel?" she whispered, captivated by the brilliance before her.

The largest of the apparitions nodded. He made the sign of the cross, and Jeanne bowed her head. She then crossed herself rapidly but kept her eyes averted, squinting from the white light.

"Do not be afraid. Rise, child."

Slowly, hesitantly, Jeanne raised her face to them, straightening up to stand proudly before them. They were no longer pulsing with brightness but had dulled enough that she could look at them without harm. Her eyes filled when she made eye contact with the two women on either side of the angel. One had hair as black as a raven's wing; the other wore a wimple so that only a reddish curl escaped near her cheek. Jeanne gasped with comprehension. She knew who they were, just as she knew it could only be Archangel Michael leading this visitation.

"Saint Catherine…Saint Margaret…"

"Arise, young maid." Catherine's clear, bell-like voice echoed in the field.

"You know who I am?" the deep male voice asked.

Jeanne nodded tentatively.

"Say it, then," he commanded.

"You are Saint Michael," Jeanne whispered.

"I am the Archangel Michael."

Jeanne paled, falling to her knees again. She looked away. "You are the angel of death. Am I to die?" she asked softly.

He smiled, shaking his head as if amused. "I am the general of the army that fights evil. I am your commander."

"My commander? The Lord is my commander. I am simply a vessel for Him to direct," she told him simply.

The male figure made the sign of the cross over her. "Yes, as I am His to command. He has ordered me to charge you with a holy task. There is to be a great war, and I am His soldier. He has given me my orders to gather an army. You shall represent me."

Jeanne quoted reverently, "And at that time shall Michael stand up, the great prince which standeth for the children of thy people: and there shall be a time of trouble, such as never was since there was a nation to that same time: and at that time thy people shall be delivered." Her words echoed in the empty garden.

"You have a calling, Jeanne d'Arc." He stepped back, allowing the two women to move forward.

"We have consecrated our virtue to Christ, our Lord. Yes, Jeanne, you too shall dedicate your life to God." Catherine's delicate, pointed finger moved in a small circle.

"Why me?" Jeanne whispered.

"The wheel of fortune has chosen you. You must follow the pattern of the wheel. Sometimes it will go up in triumph…"

"Other times," Margaret continued, "it will move down in despair. But you will never be alone."

"We died, martyred for our beliefs. Will you choose God?" Catherine bent her head, the light blindingly bright around her.

Jeanne buried her face in her hands, overcome. "What would you have me do?"

"You will lead the army and save France," Saint Michael told her.

Jeanne raised her head, her eyes incredulous. Michael was kneeling on the ground before her.

"I am dreaming. This cannot be real."

"It is real. It has been decided. You will be God's arm in France. You will inspire an army and lead it for the king. You will be the heart and soul of all the people, for in you is a pureness that is a direct conduit to God."

"I cannot lead an army. I am a girl, nothing more."

"You will be known as the Maid of Orleans. France will unite under your banner."

"But how?" Jeanne asked.

"You will drive out the English and bring the dauphin to Rheims. Because of you, the crown will be restored to France."

Jeanne stood slowly, her jaw gaping. "Me? How? I don't see how. How will I get them to listen to me?"

"Repeat after me," the angel commanded. "The Lord wills it, and this I must do."

Jeanne watched their beautiful faces. Tears sprang from her eyes, coating her cheeks. She felt the bitter salt reach her lips, and she replied, "The Lord wills it, and this I must do."

Their images became translucent, growing larger until they coalesced into a single radiant sun and then exploding into a dazzling array of stars. They disappeared with the same suddenness with which they had arrived.

Jeanne fell to the ground, sobbing. She did not know how or why, but she would have a role to play, and it would not match the one her parents had chosen for her.

Chapter 6

"Okay...okay...okay...What has this got to do with me?" Amanda slammed her computer closed with a decided snap. "I hate history. It serves no purpose," she muttered.

Nicholas turned to face her, and the breath left Amanda's body for a minute. She froze, his dark eyes impaling her. She felt trapped by his gaze. He leaned forward, the leather of his jacket making a noise as he twisted. He was inches from her face. She could feel his warm breath, her nose wrinkling from the faint odor of alcohol coming from his mouth.

"Is that you or me?" He laughed, his eyebrows raised.

Amanda recoiled.

"Oh, don't get all righteous. You probably drank as much as I did."

"How do you know what I did last night?" Amanda asked hotly. She looked contemptuously at him, noticing his jacket gaped at the shoulder as if it was ripped. She could see the white of his T-shirt and the shadow of his skin underneath. "What happened to your coat?"

Nicholas sat back, crossing his black-clad leg across his knee, ignoring her. He rested his large hand on his ankle but moved his leg restlessly, bouncing it. Amanda reached out to touch him impatiently. He made her more nervous. "Stop that," she said.

"Why?"

"Because it's annoying."

"And your point is?" Nicholas turned to face her.

Amanda sat back abruptly.

"See?" Nicholas said with a satisfied air. "You don't know what the point is. So why don't you open up your computer and figure it out?"

Amanda twisted to look at the exit. The row of doors taunted her. She rose and gathered her things quickly.

"I wouldn't if I were you." Nick watched her intently. His brown eyes pinned her. Again, she had the feeling she knew him. "Look at the door."

Amanda glanced up. The gloved fists were back, pounding at the entrance. The outline of a face pressed against the glass, the eyes black holes in the grayish skin. A dark hat was pulled low, but the features were still discernible. The face was hideous, lined as if carved by a rake, the thick skin a pulsing, purplish flesh, as if it spent its time underground. The gloved hands had long fingers, solid and strong, that could never have belonged to any human she knew. Amanda stood frozen, her heart beating like a trapped bird, her feet frozen with fear.

A scream bubbled up from her throat, and Nick tugged her back into her seat. She fell with a plop, his cold hand imprisoning her wrist. Her thoughts skittered in her mind, as if a great wind were pushing them. The image of the man in the rear dissolved, to be replaced by her irritation at the class. Amanda wondered for a second what had unnerved her but couldn't recall the reason. She faced Nick. "This has nothing to do with me!" she whispered fiercely.

"It has everything to do with you."

"No, it doesn't," Amanda said stubbornly. "She was a crazy girl who claimed visions told her she was going to lead France in the Hundred Years' War. I don't need to know any more than that."

"You think so," Nick said with a patience that made her teeth grit. "People are trapped in history, and history is trapped in them."

"That's just about the stupidest thing I've ever heard. The only thing I'm trapped in is this dumb lecture. I know what happened to Joan. I learned all about it in Sunday school. She united France under some French king with an enormous nose and got captured, and then they burned her at the stake for being a cross-dresser," she said.

A loud clapping rent the room. Amanda looked up, startled, to see the teacher standing on the stage, his large hands making the noise. "Brava, Miss Greene. You know everything. You don't need to be here." He gestured to the exit. "Be my guest."

Amanda eyed the back of the hall nervously. Her feet wouldn't budge; her tush was glued to the seat. Amanda went rigid with indecision. The room was like a vacuum, completely silent. A lone trickle of sweat made its way from her hairline. She needed a Lifesaver. Pushing her hands deep into her pockets, she fished around for a peppermint candy. The cellophane crinkled loudly in the auditorium.

"It's so much more than that," Nick said harshly.

Amanda popped the candy into her mouth. The taste, the smell of it reminded her of Patrick. It calmed her. She looked at the professor, as if she was considering something, then shrugged indifferently. Her mind was made up. She stuffed her laptop into her bag.

Nick whispered, his face pleading, "You should stay."

Amanda's eyes narrowed at the professor. Nick smiled and said, "Oh, him? His bark is much worse than his bite. He's just a means to the end."

"The end to what?"

"You'll have to finish the class to find out."

Frustration simmered in her taut body. She looked at the door and then at Nick's impassive face, her feelings warring with indecision. She scanned the lecture hall. The students were all facing front, like robots. Amanda groaned and sat ungracefully into her seat. She yanked open her laptop.

"Since you know the story," the professor said sarcastically, "we shall try not to bore you with unnecessary details." He raised his eyebrows, his face diabolical in the muted light. "Are we ready, Miss Greene?"

It was only after he started the lecture that Amanda realized he knew her name.

CHAPTER 7

France, 1430

The cell was dank and cold, with moldy green moss growing on the walls. Water dripped somewhere. She had been given back her male attire. Jeanne had complained to the priest that the soldiers had tried to rape her, as had the English lord. She counted three times they had attempted to relieve her of her virtue, but she had fought hard, taking a beating as vicious as she gave it. They had pulled at her skirts, ripping, squeezing. She was safer in boys' clothing, even if it was blasphemous. The church had finally relented, allowing her to wear the hosen, boots, and tunic. She was supposed to be guarded by nuns. Hers was a religious offense, yet the English locked her in with soldiers.

Jeanne sighed. She had scaled the walls of the last prison from an opening and had fallen over sixty feet in her escape, and she was now in an impenetrable tower in Rouen. There were no windows in her new prison.

Jeanne fell on her knees and rested her face against the damp floor. There was talk, floating whispers that her allies were planning an attack. They would save her. She had heard that her army was massing, getting ready to liberate her. It was impossible, though; nobody could win. She knew her destiny, had known it since that fateful day on her father's farm. She was unafraid. Jeanne had faced an army in little more than the white armor gifted to her by the king and had felt no fear. God was at her back. She would go to her death knowing she honored Him as well as herself. She had not given them what they wanted; she would never give in. The whole trial was a mockery, anyway. Jeanne shrugged. They had not allowed her a legal advisor. The court was stacked against her, she had protested. The tribunal was heavily biased, pro-English. She had argued for French clergy to be present but was ignored.

Jeanne had stunned them. She smiled serenely, outwitting them with clever answers they had never expected from a country maid. It didn't matter. Whatever she said, no one really heard. In the end, no one was listening to her.

It was over now. She was guilty, guilty for standing true to her beliefs and following her destiny.

They led her to her pyre. Fire surrounded her, licking at her. "Jesus," she cried, "Jesus, Jesus…" Jeanne called for salvation and an end to her misery. The fire consumed her, filling her until she exploded into a million small sparks of energy. Those sparks reached out to singe the world.

CHAPTER 8

Amanda bit back a small scream, a memory rushing into her head like a tsunami, wrapping itself around her brain. She gripped her skull, a pounding, roaring storm ripping through her brain, emptying it of reality and replacing it with an image, the searing of intense heat, the stench of burning hair.

The fire-hot breath scorched her, bathing her face until sweat broke out on her forehead, dripping down her heated cheeks. Wayne held her hand over the scalding coils of the radiator. The steam hissed, and he grabbed the back of her skull, forcing her face inches from the hot surface. Amanda heard the boiling water gurgle in the pipes; her hair sparked with static. Her nose filled with snot, her tearing eyes wide in her paralyzed face. Heat from the pipes shimmered before her eyes, smothering her.

"See what will happen if you tell? I'll burn you."

Amanda made a fist and brought it upward to smack Wayne in his groin. He fell to the floor, releasing her with a groan. He cupped his crotch, howling, and then kicked out, catching her in the knee, hitting her so hard that tears sprang to her eyes. She landed in a heap. He swung out, but she rolled, eluding his fist.

"I don't like you, Wayne."

"You don't have to like me, Mandy. You just have to make me happy." He scrambled on the rug, hooking her arm, attempting to roll on top of her. He smiled tightly, struggling with her flailing arms.

Amanda pulled her arm out of his grip and retreated to the corner of the living room, away from the heat of the radiator. She rubbed her wrist where Wayne had gripped her. She glanced down; a red ring braceleted her wrist.

"Hurts?" Wayne taunted. He snickered at her. At fifteen he was not only four years older but double her size.

"I'm gonna tell," Amanda told him, her face angry.

The teen took the wrought-iron fireplace poker and hefted it from hand to hand.

"Yeah, crybaby? What are you gonna say?" he taunted.

Amanda made a move, but Wayne feinted, cutting her off. She darted in the other direction, but he grabbed her sweater. She resisted, and he pulled hard, his manhandling stretching the material so that it nearly covered her entire hand. Amanda banged into the lamp and watched in horror as it wobbled and then fell.

Wayne laughed and threw the poker against the wall, making a big black mark.

"Ouch, Manda, stop!" he shouted, his face watching hers with malice.

Amanda's mother rushed into the room, her face filled with anger. Her shadowed eyes zeroed in on her daughter, who now stood defiantly beside the shattered lamp.

"Amanda!" she shouted, grabbing the broken lamp by its shade. "What's going on in here?"

"I tried to warn her she was too rough, Natalie. Look." Wayne walked over to the poker by the broken sheetrock. "I told her not to throw that."

Amanda's mother placed her hands on her hips, her face warm and inviting. "Wayne, I told you—call me Mom. I thought we had that worked out." She turned to Amanda, her eyes narrowing. "Why can't you get along? What's wrong with you?"

Amanda bit her bottom lip, her eyes lowered. She didn't like Wayne—or her mother's new husband, Albert. She had asked to move in with her dad, but he was in Asia on business, relocated with his new wife. She only saw him in the summer, and this past July he had canceled because they were not settled in yet. He didn't want to upset Claudine—she was pregnant, after all. Nana had offered to take her but met a lot of resistance from Mom. With their move to Florida, and flights so expensive, now Amanda only saw her grandparents at Christmas, if she was lucky.

Wayne placed the poker in its stand. He threw himself into the corner of the sectional, struggling with the lever on the side to raise the footrest. It appeared broken. He shrugged. "I told her not to be too rough with it."

Natalie frowned. "If you broke the new couch, I don't know what I am going to do. Sometimes, Amanda, I don't understand..."

The teen yanked the lever hard, his small muscles bulging. Amanda watched stone faced as his strong hands twisted the wood. She knew those hurtful, probing hands. She looked up to her mother, revulsion rising when she saw her pleased face observing Wayne.

"It's so nice to have not just one but two men around the house again. Huh, Mandy?" her mother said with a stupid grin.

The couch groaned loudly. The footrest popped out, and a headless doll flew from the confined place. Amanda felt tears sting her eyes. It was her favorite, given to her by her grandmother.

Her mother slapped her hard. "Jesus, Manda!" she yelled. "Can't you take care of anything? Nana bought you that doll in Europe." Natalie swiped it up and examined the tortured limbs with disgust. The eyes were gouged out, one arm had been burned to the elbow, and there was a gaping hole where the belly button was supposed to be.

Amanda looked over her mother's bent form, making eye contact with Wayne. He smirked, pursing his lips in an obscene mockery of a kiss. Natalie stood, lifted Amanda by the arm impatiently, and dragged her from the room. She whipped her into a corner in the kitchen.

"What is wrong with you?" she demanded. The pasta chose that inconvenient time to boil over. Natalie cursed and then muttered to herself worriedly, "He hates when it's overcooked." She pulled the strainer from the boiling water. It splashed, sending a dart of heat to smack Amanda in the cheek. It singed her skin as if a needle had pricked her, bringing tears to her green eyes. Natalie moved the dripping pot into the sink, oblivious that she had burned her daughter.

Amanda wiped her cheek hastily, staring stonily at her mother, her lips trembling. She opened her mouth to say something, but her mother spoke over her angrily. "If you ruin this, I swear I'll send you away to Thailand, and you won't see me, your friends, or even Nana for a long—"

"Myanmar."

"What?" Natalie said impatiently.

"Myanmar. It's not Thailand. It used to be Burma, and they changed it—"

"Who cares!" Natalie exploded. "He's gone, and Nana's gone, and you are only left with me! Albert, Wayne, and *me*!" She pointed her wet finger close to Amanda's face. "And now he's going to be very busy with the stewardess and their love child."

"Can't be a love child. They got married."

"Enough, Amanda! It doesn't matter. It's ancient history, and it's over. Besides, you couldn't have liked living in that crappy apartment," her mother's shrill voice whispered. "Stop acting like a martyr, or I swear." Natalie dropped the colander into the sink, suddenly exhausted. "You're not Joan of Arc, you know. It will get better, Amanda. You have to get used to sharing me, is all."

Amanda stood woodenly, her mouth sealed, her heart on fire. She missed Nana. Nana understood. Nana loved her. She hardly ever saw Nana and Papa Joe anymore, not since Albert had come into the picture. When her grandparents visited, they had to stay at a motel. They made him uncomfortable, Albert said, his new in-laws. Still, she had been able to fly to Florida this past summer and escape Wayne for a few weeks. Nana had asked what was wrong. Amanda closed her mouth, her tongue clamped tightly against her teeth. She couldn't tell, not anyone. She was afraid, embarrassed and afraid. She felt small and alone. She looked toward the living room, where the sound of the television competed with Wayne's laughter. She studied her mother, busy placing hamburgers on a platter, chopped vegetables on another. She had to tell her; she couldn't do this anymore. Wayne was getting more aggressive.

"He touches me," Amanda whispered.

Natalie poured sauce over the vegetables, working quickly and efficiently.

Amanda cleared her throat. "Mom…he…"

"I hated being single," Natalie mused. She spoke a one-sided conversation, looking at her reflection in the glass window above the sink. "It's hard to raise a daughter alone—not that two is so easy, but Wayne is a nice kid. He's on the honor roll. I love when he reads to you." She turned to stare hard at her daughter. "He's such a nice boy. Come on, Amanda, why do I have to do it all? Can't you help a little bit here?" She stared out the kitchen window, lost in a memory. "I'm so tired of struggling."

Amanda moved close, hiding her face in the side of her mother's shirt. She smelled her soft cologne. Her mother's hand inched out to pull Amanda against her. "I just want to make us a better life, Amanda. I can't do this alone."

"Mommy, he touches me." Amanda's voice was muffled by her mother's shirt.

Natalie turned and cupped Amanda's face in her wet palms. "He's a boy, and he's playful. He loves you like a brother should. You are not used to it. Don't let your imagination run away with you."

Amanda looked up at her mother, hope dying. Her mother didn't believe her. Nobody would believe her. Her lips compressed into a tight line, her insides shrinking until they squeezed into a tight knot.

The door opened, and Albert yelled a warm greeting. Natalie sighed with relief.

A small spark ignited under Amanda's breastbone, sizzling and singeing organs, burning flesh, consuming her heart. The fire raged, consuming the little girl, leaving nothing but the ashes of her innocence in its wake.

"Go on, then." Natalie smiled. "Go say hello to your father."

Chapter 9

Amanda slammed her laptop shut with a curse. "This is stupid." She didn't realize she had said it out loud until she noticed the silence in the vast auditorium. She looked up, astonished to see a sea of faces observing her. She squirmed with unease from her flashback. She turned to Nick, shaking her head. "I don't want to do this." Before he could answer, she rose, her heart beating rapidly in her chest, her cheeks bright red with embarrassment and anger. Her chest burned as if a fire raged there. She considered the exit. What bothered her about going out there was that she couldn't recall anything but the feeling of unease, as if there was some sort of threat in the darkness beyond the door.

She had had enough. She'd rather face whatever frightened her outside than deal with this crap in here. Besides that, Nick was decidedly weird. She stomped her way down the row, her backside brushing against the parade of knees. The aisle looked endless. She began her dash to the exit sign. The passage stretched before her, growing steeper by the minute, but she pushed on, her calf muscles screaming in protest. The rug bunched under her feet, and a spark of panic ignited in her chest again when she realized it felt as if she were slogging her way through a swamp. Her breathing became labored, sweat beading her brow. She pushed on, stopping wearily and checking her distance from the stage to the way out. It appeared farther rather than closer. Amanda started running, her legs heavy, her arms heavy, the room so weighted with silence that it hurt her ears. She heard panicked breaths and was soon gulping both her sobs and the thick air into her constricted lungs. She leaped onto the landing and rested her hands on her knees, only to find the exit was somehow even further away. The door was a small pinprick of light in the distance. Amanda sobbed loudly. Her breathing labored, she ran desperately, watching the many faces blur as she sprinted toward freedom. No sooner had she gotten to her destination than the door appeared on the other side of the room. She had to find Patrick; he would make her feel safe.

On the stage, the teacher steamed up like a teapot, his body quivering with rage.

"Really." He drew out the one word with dripping scorn. He stomped to the center, his sandals flipping loudly against the stage. His voice rang out, halting her escape. "You obnoxious, impudent weasel." He pointed a beringed finger at her. "You tiresome spoiled brat, you overbearing—"

Amanda spun to face his wrath, tears leaking from the corners of her eyes. What kind of hell was she in?

"Professor, you have to give her a learning curve." Nick was standing, the gaping hole in his jacket even wider now.

"You want me to spoon-feed her as well, Mr. Fortune?"

"Come back," Nick called to her. He gazed at the teacher on the stage. "You know how hard this is. After all, it's logical that she doesn't understand." He turned to face her, his hand held out to her, his palm up. His face had softened, had lost the hard angles. "It could have been worse," he told her with a grin. "You could have gotten Socrates."

"Oh," a girl said from the seat to her left. "He's a dead bore. You're much better off here. Go sit down."

The teacher laughed, his great belly shaking so hard that it dislodged the top of his toga, which fell, revealing a broad chest covered with curly gray hair. The room erupted with laughter. The professor looked down, his face alight with merriment.

"Perhaps you are right, young Fortune," he wheezed. "Shall we try this again?" He looked in question to Amanda, who stared back with frightened confusion. The teacher sighed wearily. "You don't even realize who I am, do you? Besides, you don't really want to go outside, do you?" He pointed to the exit.

The face was back, pressing its distorted features into the glass, its mouth open in a soundless scream. It looked like the creature in the Munch painting.

Nick walked toward her, but she eased out of his grip, eyeing him with distrust. He shrugged with a wry smile and motioned her to follow him back to their seats. She walked after him, feeling like a sheep, as though he had some kind of influence over her that she wasn't comfortable with. Still, being with him kept her away from the figure pounding on the door.

"Forget about him," he said dismissively. He tapped her shoulder.

Once Nick touched her, all coherent thought fled. Oddly enough, she did forget about the threat at the door. Amanda reluctantly walked back to her seat.

"She'll figure it all out soon enough," Nick assured the professor.

The teacher shrugged. "Some do. Some don't."

Nick led her to her seat and said, "This is all about association. Do you remember? The whole idea is that memories are triggered by association. It always is frightening the first time."

She stared blankly at him, and the crowd shifted in their seats.

"I am not associating anything with Jeanne d'Arc," Amanda whined.

The teacher shouted, "She's as dense as a plank of wood."

"It's simple, Amanda. It has nothing to do with Jeanne. Think about it. It's about the image. You see an image or read something, and it will trigger a memory."

"For what purpose?" she asked, her eyes wide with fear. She touched her cheek where the boiling pasta water burned her in her mother's kitchen seven years ago.

The professor threw up his hands with frustration. "I always said we shouldn't include the girls."

Amanda looked longingly for the exit, realizing with a start she couldn't find it anymore. She heard Nick say, "You'll find it when you're ready. Stop worrying about it and pay attention."

The professor interrupted them. "All right, open your books to page eight thousand seven hundred forty-three."

There was a communal groan. "That's right," the teacher said snidely. "We are going to have a little chat about Lucrezia Borgia."

CHAPTER 10

Men become accustomed to poison by degrees.

—Victor Hugo

Rome, 1483

"'Tis unnatural, Maria. I cannot abide by it." The nursery maid huffed as she stuffed the linens in the chest.

"Hush. Do you want to be thrown out?" The older maid looked behind them with a warning in her eyes. "Or worse, even. His Eminence's red robes are powerful. Shut your mouth and close your eyes. You are not paid to notice things." She pulled the younger maid from the room, pausing only to dip a deep curtsy to the cardinal, who sat sprawled in his chair.

A child sat before him on a small stool, her wheaten locks spread across the red robes like a blanket as he brushed his daughter's hair.

"Bellissima," he crooned. "I shall make you a great match for me one day, my little beauty."

Tears gathered in the child's hazel eyes. She sniffed loudly, her full lips pouting. He turned her to face him, his own eyes warm with love. "What is it, my dove?"

She climbed onto his lap, heedless of his dignity, and curled against his chest, her pudgy hands playing with the great silver crucifix on his chest.

"I miss Mama. I want to go home."

"This is your home now, little one." He lifted her chin with his hand.

Lucrezia's breath caught in her chest. He was so handsome, her papa, Rodrigo Borgia, the famous cardinal. He had deep-set eyes and a strong nose. She pulled it playfully. Lucrezia had his mouth—and his gift for captivating an audience as well. Soon both his name and position would change. Big things were planned for him. He had chosen the name Alexander, like the conqueror, for the coming election. Not yet, but soon, he told her. They had to prepare for the great things in their future. He stroked her cheek, and she purred like a cat. She loved it when he gave her attention, any attention.

"I don't understand, Papa. I want to live with Mama."

Rodrigo Borgia clicked his tongue and then tweaked her nose indulgently. "*Cara*, I have many things planned for you and your brothers. I cannot do these things for you if you live with your mama."

"But why?" she wheedled. Things had been so nice when she lived with Mama and her brothers. They had so much fun. Papa was never far, and when he came bearing presents and fine clothes, they behaved like a little family. She didn't have to think about the fact that he didn't live with them all the time. After all, he was a very important man.

"It's because we are bastards." Cesare's words earned him a very nasty slap from Papa. Because of his big mouth, they had been removed from Mama's house to come and live with Papa's cousins. Lucrezia pouted, and Rodrigo flicked her ear.

Lucrezia squealed with dismay. "I don't like that," she snapped.

Rodrigo roared with laughter. "You have such spirit, little one. You keep that spirit, and don't let anyone take it away from you."

Lucrezia frowned, her hazel eyes filling.

"Come now, Lucrezia. You'll ruin your beauty, and then where will I be? Stuck with an ugly little girl and no prospects for a good marriage. Mama understands, and you will too when you get older."

He pulled her against his chest, squeezing her fiercely. "Nobody loves you like me. I will do anything for you."

"And I will do anything for you, Papa," the little girl said earnestly.

He took her head in both his hands and kissed her on both cheeks. "You remember, child. You are my favorite."

"Juan is your favorite. He is oldest."

Rodrigo frowned, and his eyes narrowed. Lucrezia eyed her father speculatively. She walked her fingers up his chest, causing him to watch her intently. She was an imp. He smiled indulgently.

"Is Cesare your favorite, Papa?" Lucrezia asked innocently. "I will tell you a secret." She leaned up, her sweet baby's breath tickling his ear. "He is my favorite." The cardinal reared back, his face comically turned down. "After you, of course, Papa."

Rodrigo stood and threw her high in the air. "You will be a great lady when the time comes, my little minx." He hugged her tightly and then set her down, his mind already on his great position and the problems left waiting for his attention in his papal office.

CHAPTER 11

Amanda tapped her pen against the metal bottom of her seat, her mind on a clock ticking in her head. If she tried, she couldn't recount what the teacher was nattering on about. Who cared about some pope and his illegitimate child? For the few hours they had spent learning about Joan of Arc, all she remembered was searing heat and the despicable memories of her molestation as a child. How that was supposed to relate to anything she had heard, she still hadn't figured out. Professor Aristotle gave her a hard look and paused with a sigh. He said, "I'll give you all one hour." He rubbed his face, his fingers threading in his beard, and then turned to walk out of the room.

Sighs of relief rushed through the room.

Amanda stood, stretching her cramped muscles. "I thought he'd never finish."

Nick rose, swinging a worn leather backpack over his shoulder. "Want coffee?"

Amanda nodded shyly, marveling at how easily she moved up the aisle toward the exit. She looked back at the stage, wondering why it didn't seem far. As they approached the row of doors, a dart of apprehension made her legs wobble. Nick turned and took her elbow to escort her outside. She couldn't explain why his touch made her pull away, but her skin crawled, and she jerked backward, falling into another student. Amanda apologized, relieved that it didn't seem to bother Nick at all.

The sun was at its zenith, and Amanda watched varied students stop to talk in clusters. Some sprawled in the grass, and others started a Frisbee game. The volume of the babble of a thousand voices was both familiar and comforting. She felt as if she were leaving a concert.

She heard snatches of conversation, names mentioned with wonder. Heated discussions.

"I don't understand why he is dedicating the whole class to Jesse James."

"Who ever heard of Robert Yeates? I mean, I get that the can opener changed history…"

"Al Jolson…seriously…Al freaking Jolson…What is he thinking?"

They pushed their way through the small groups, Amanda's ears picking up more names than she could imagine. Tolstoy, Paul Walker, Mozart, Henry the Eighth, Columbus, Hank Aaron—it seemed as vast as it was varied. Nick came up to stroll beside her, his ever-alert eyes watching the surroundings.

"Do you hear them? Did we all just come from the same lecture?" she asked. She looked at Nick searchingly.

He shrugged indifferently. "What did you hear?"

"In there? Some crap about Joan of Arc, and for no apparent rhyme or reason, he launched into the childhood of Lucrezia Borgia. And his stupid costume—*Aristotle*, for God's sake. Does he think it enhances the educational experience?"

"Stay close to me." He looked around, his eyes scanning their surroundings.

Amanda shivered. She followed his gaze nervously.

She watched Nick ease through the crowd, Patrick's face filling her head. She toyed with the mints in her pocket, feeling her fingers crush them into powder. Impatiently she removed her hands. She pushed Patrick's image away. It wasn't as though she were interested in Nick or anything. They shared the same class. She looked around guiltily. It felt wrong to walk with him. In fact, something about him made her decidedly uncomfortable. Her flesh burned between her shoulder blades, as if the hard stares of onlookers were boring a hole into her back. She stole a glance at Nick, feeling out of step. She didn't belong with him. Her heart lay heavy in her chest, Patrick on her mind. Her insides were raw with longing; a piece of a puzzle was missing, a gaping black hole was left. Usually she and Pat talked after a fight. This time, nothing. Not even a call. Well, maybe he had called and she didn't know. Her phone was crushed, after all. And missing. At this point, after the blowout yesterday, she was sure she and Patrick were done. Regret filled her heart. She wanted to be alone. She took a resentful sideways glance at Nick. He seemed intent on his trek. People didn't look at him, acknowledge him. In fact, they kept a distance. It unnerved her. He didn't smile much. Well, neither did she, for that matter.

They walked the path and came to a fork. She paused, staring at the two roads. Nick walked purposefully to the left.

He stopped, his hands deep in his jacket. "It's this way." It looked overcast, dark and foreboding.

Amanda sighed heavily, her mind on Patrick. "I don't know." She looked backward fretfully.

Nick turned inward, seemingly lost in thought, and left her to walk slowly up the path.

Amanda watched him move farther away. The wind blew gustily, turning her bones to ice. The gusts howled like a panther scream. Shivering, she hurried after him.

They rounded a curve that led to an outdoor pavilion that spread out in cement circles. Umbrellaed tables in the school colors polka-dotted the patios. A line snaked out the open door.

Amanda decided to make conversation. "How can you take that guy seriously when he makes a mockery of his lesson? Dressing up in a costume. Hah."

They grabbed a couple of mocha soy lattes and then slid into a deserted table. They drank in unhurried silence. She noticed Nick didn't say much, though his eyes were constantly roaming the landscape, watching, watchful. Amanda collected the garbage that was left and walked to a trash can in the middle of the lawn. She heard Nick call her name worriedly.

She turned, a smile on her face. "Relax, the trash is right here." She pointed to the can a few feet away on the lawn.

She trudged on, the ground mushy under her feet, slowing her progress. She looked around for evidence of rain, noticing this area was absurdly quiet. Not even a bird chirped. Her skin prickled with alarm, and she paused, turning a half circle. Something made her breath quicken. She heard it. Someone called, a low, throaty sound whispering her name. It danced on the air, wrapping itself around her, making her heart beat slowly, until all she heard was the deep intake of her lungs as they inhaled. She blinked, and a fog rolled in, covering the coffee shop, the scenery becoming muted, blurry.

A hand lightly touched her shoulder, setting off sparks. She gasped, turning, but whoever had caressed her was gone. The wind tickled her hair, pulling at the auburn curls until they bounced around her face. A fatigue washed through her body, making her knees tremble, her arms becoming almost too heavy. She rubbed her eyes, yawning, lassitude filling her entire being. A gentle caress rolled across her back, coming to rest upon her hip. She recognized the heaviness of possession, surprised at her inability to care. A warm breath fanned her ear, whispering her name lovingly, inviting her to a seduction. A lazy smile graced her fine lips. The large brim of a dark hat shielded his face, but when Amanda looked up, her eyes opened in horror at the gaping maw facing her. The gray face, the skin thick as putty, with empty holes for eyes, stared back at her with a mirthless jack-o'-lantern grin. A cold hand with rubbery fingers moved to clutch her neck, cutting off the air, so her scream ended in a soundless whimper. Amanda felt a heavy weight pushing her straight down, as if she were being screwed into the earth vertically, her ankles encased in mud, her hand gripping the slimy hands that were now squeezing her neck.

Struggling, she twisted, trying to pull her trapped feet from the prison of the mud, but they were held tight. She heard triumphant laughter, the sound bouncing through her fading consciousness. Bells were ringing, and she became aware of distant beeping, clanging sirens, lights flashing, but he held on, swinging her body like a boneless carcass. Amanda tried unsuccessfully to suck in breath, the blue sky fading to a tiny pinprick.

Something banged into the two of them. Amanda's starved lungs sucked in great gulps of air. She was thrown to the hard ground, her attacker yanked off. She rolled over, her eyes dully watching Nick wrestling with the larger figure, the black, billowing coat swirling in the wind.

She shivered, remembering the tight hold on her neck. The tall figure had Nick in a bear hold. She couldn't see anything but the darkness of the man, his oversized coat flapping like bats' wings. Amanda's strength surged, pumping adrenaline through her veins. Struggling to her feet, she roared and leaped onto his back, holding on and punching him in the kidneys. It was like hitting stone. She heard the sound of flesh being pounded, a flurry of fists, followed by deep grunts. She pulled at the dark hat seemingly glued onto her attacker's head. She ripped it off with triumph, only to stare stunned at the purplish, hairless surface of his head. He looked like a putrid hard-boiled egg.

Nick's fist connected with the side of his face, and the coat dissolved into dust, becoming a foul swarm of bees, a black cloud that covered the sky. The wall of insects flew upward in a solid mass that obliterated light. They did a strange ballet, looping around the horizon and then blinking out of sight. Amanda landed on the grass with a hard thud. Her elbow connected with a rock, hitting the peculiar spot called the funny bone, making her eyes water, leading her to wonder what fool in *history* had named it that.

"I told you to stay close to me," Nick said breathlessly.

Amanda nursed her sore elbow. "What?" she croaked. "What happened? Where is he? It? Whatever?" She scrambled to her feet. "Where's the call box? I have to report this to security."

"Forget it." Nick waved a hand. "You can't do anything about it." He looked at his cell, noting the time. "We have to get back, anyway."

"Are you kidding me? This place is nuts!" Amanda stomped away from him. "Who was that guy?"

"You wouldn't believe me if I told you."

"I'm going to the admin building. Someone's got to do something."

"Don't you get it?" Nick grabbed her arm. "Nobody can help you. You are the only one who can help you."

Amanda snatched her hand away, rubbing it where Nick had held her. She felt contaminated from him. She angrily picked up her bag, ignoring Nick as she walked in the direction of her dorm.

"Amanda," Nick shouted. "Come back."

Amanda stormed off, the sudden stillness of the atmosphere, the absence of birds gelling the air. She stopped, her breath ragged. She heard the familiar whisper of her name, the cold chill of it dancing down her spine. Amanda spun and ran to the safety of Nick's companionship. Though they walked together, she kept her distance, her head warily watching the surroundings.

CHAPTER 12

"I don't think we're in Kansas anymore," Amanda said quietly as they trudged back to the auditorium.

"We're not in Kansas," Nick said. "We're in—"

"It was a joke," Amanda said impatiently. "You know, from *The Wizard of Oz.* Look, Nick. Something weird is going on here." She reached out to touch his jacket lightly. "Are you for real? Did I dream you up?"

Nick brushed off her hand and then said sullenly, "We'll be late." The crowd had thinned. People were climbing the steps, returning to the lecture hall.

"Wait!" Amanda's shout stopped him. "At least tell me something so I don't think I'm having a breakdown."

Nick bit the inside of his cheek, his face impassive.

Amanda's brain raced. "Am I dead?" she asked desperately.

Nick gave a barely perceptible negative shake.

"Then what? Dreaming? Give me something, Nick!"

"I can't," he replied, his lips barely moving.

Amanda studied his closed face. He avoided her gaze, his brown eyes downcast.

"They're all hearing the same lecture, right?" Amanda asked tentatively.

"They all hear what they have to hear."

"Oh, that makes a lot of sense." She threw up her hands.

Nick leaned over, the rip in his jacket wider, a crimson stain on his white tee.

"Oh my God, are you hurt?"

He shook his head again. "It's an old injury."

Amanda eyed him doubtfully.

"Look, I would tell you if I could. I can't."

Amanda heaved a sigh of frustration. She pursed her lips, her eyes looking everywhere but at him.

Nick shifted and then said, "You have to trust me. Finish the lecture."

"With Plato?" She shook her head. She didn't trust him or Aristotle or whatever was happening to her. Nick was simply the lesser of two evils. At least he wasn't as irritating as the singing roommate.

He smiled tentatively, almost as if he didn't know how. His mouth wobbled, and she felt a great well of sadness coming from him. She noticed a fan shape of fine lines at the corner of his eyes and wondered if she had misjudged his age.

"You know who it is. You've known all along. You play at being the dumb one, but…" He looked around worriedly. "You've got to finish this."

"I didn't know I had started anything."

He shook his head, his lips a tight line. A buzzer sounded, and he headed to the entrance of the auditorium.

Amanda stood bleakly at the base of the steps. Nick turned and looked down at her, his face impassive. He pivoted wordlessly and entered the glass doors.

Amanda searched the distance for the white clapboard of the registrar's office, but a dense fog obscured the green hills. She gazed in the other direction for her dorm building. Nothing was there but a gray sky that threatened rain. The wind whistled eerily, and she heard the flapping of material, the dark coat. With a shriek, she ran up the steps. Nick stood in the doorway, his eyes watching the horizon. He held the door open, and Amanda scurried in wordlessly. Nick nodded once, his face impassive, and they walked down the aisle to their seats.

Chapter 13

He was standing behind the lectern, his deep-set eyes watching Amanda as she followed Nick to their places. When his lips turned upward in a grin, Amanda shivered with revulsion. His expression bordered on contempt. She stared up at him defiantly, and he chuckled, laughing at her without humor.

"Is he really…"

Nick's set face caused her mouth to close. She slid into her chair, her movements shadowing her mentor. *Her mentor*, she thought. She was supposed to get a mentor the first week. Amanda turned to say something, but the lecture began, and Nick's stony gaze made the words dry on her tongue, unsaid.

Rome, 1495

Cesare Borgia stalked into the papal apartments, a dark scowl on his lean, wolfish face. His narrow, dark eyes surveyed the crowded room, his lips thin with impatience. "It's a cesspit out there." He threw a pair of studded leather riding gloves onto a side table inlaid with precious gems. The color of his cardinal's robes appeared bloodred in the dim interior of the quarters. His black hair curled at his temples and fell in a cascade down his back.

Juan leaned against the wall, a tapestry of General Holofernes's assassination with the biblical heroine Judith proudly holding his dismembered head. He turned to caress the jewel threads of the artwork. "Twenty-three murders this week alone," he said to his father, the pope.

Pope Alexander VI, the former Rodrigo Borgia, turned his dark gaze upon his oldest son. "You say that as if it makes you proud."

"It's not my fault you can't make the assorted families get along. They squabble like children, while the French raid us."

"The enemy is at our gates!" Cesare lunged at his brother Juan, grabbing the white ruffles worn under his velvet jerkin. Cesare's red cardinal's robes contrasted with Juan's black doublet.

"I did not invite France here," Juan spat, his deep-set eyes so like his father's, fiery with hatred.

"Well, Captain-General, if you had spent less time in Violetta's bed and more time at the head of your troops, we wouldn't have to worry about Charles and his army."

There was a gasp, and both men were distracted by two girls sitting on the window seat. Julia Farnese, the pope's mistress, sat playing cat's cradle with his daughter Lucrezia. They were a study in opposites; Lucrezia was fair and open, and Giulia la Bella a dark, mysterious seductress. The string hung limply from the younger girl's hands, her face gleaming white in the gloom. At fifteen, she was stunningly beautiful, married to her father's ally, and one of the most powerful women of her time. But she was still a child—spoiled, petted, and indulged by her entire family.

Alexander laid his quill down decisively and then walked over and separated his two eldest sons. "They are disloyal because I have taken lands in the north and given them to you, Cesare. They feel as though I am robbing them of their possessions."

Cesare threw himself onto a chair, his long legs spread out before him.

"Have you seen my husband?" Lucrezia ran over to kneel at his feet. "Have you? Did he say anything? He is not taking me home? Did he say anything, Cesare?" Her pale face looked up at him with alarm.

Cesare's dark eyes softened. He took a long blond curl and twirled it on his elegant finger, threading it around his gold-and-amethyst ecclesiastical ring. He stared hard at the jewel, the heavy weight of it crushing his finger. He hated it. He clicked his tongue upon noticing his sister's tear-washed eyes.

"She's a brat," Juan brayed. "Sforza is coming to take you back to Pesaro, my great lady. It's time you made him an heir."

Lucrezia looked up at her father with a panicked face, her lips bloodless. "No, Papa, you promised I wouldn't have to go." She scrambled to her feet to latch on to her father's white robes. "I said I'd be good. You said I could stay here…with you…and Giulia. I will do anything to stay here with you, Papa."

Cesare bounded up to grab his brother, but the pope got there before him, slapping Juan on his face. "Leave, fool, else I switch your brother's papal robes with your fine military uniform and let your brother lead my army."

Juan drew himself up with furious dignity, snatched his sword from where it stood leaning against the wall, and stormed from the room.

"Leave, you pox-ridden, pestilent whoreson." Lucrezia ran after him, smacking the back of his head.

Alexander chuckled. "Shame, daughter. Such poison falling from your lips. Giulia." He reached around to pull his mistress close to him. "How did this come about? Who taught my little princess this filth?"

Giulia's round face directed her dark eyes at Cesare, a mischievous smile on her full lips. "The devil himself."

"Papa," Lucrezia interrupted. "You promised I wouldn't ever have to go back with that beast again." She climbed onto his lap coyly.

Alexander kissed her forehead tenderly while he exchanged a look with his son. "Go play, child." He placed her firmly on the floor.

"I don't want to leave." Lucrezia stuck out her lower lip petulantly.

Alexander motioned for them to return to the window seat. Cesare joined him at his desk.

"What troubles you?"

Cesare looked around the room, his face suspicious. He walked to the door and opened it rapidly, satisfying himself that no one was there.

He pulled a packet of letters from underneath his shirt and dropped them onto his father's desk. "It was the Orsinis," he said with deadly calm.

The pope sighed, his hand rubbing his brow. "I don't believe it. Giambattista swayed the vote to get me elected pope. I made him papal legate of Ancona," he whispered in disbelief.

Cesare took a dagger from his boot and slammed the tip though the papers, pinning them to the desk. "Well, Your Grace, he's in bed with the French. You should have made me captain-general. Juan will never be able to take control of them. If you let them ally themselves with Charles, it is only a matter of time before more families follow. We have to crush this betrayal this now!"

Alexander tapped his fingers on the desk.

Cesare leaned close, his voice a hiss. The women sat giggling in the window seat. Giulia parted the heavy drapes so that molten sunlight bathed Lucrezia's face, gilding her in gold. Cesare looked up, his predatory eyes observing her.

"You dine tonight with Orsini's cousin. He advises Giambattista. He protects the land to the west of the Orsini castle."

Alexander warned, "Do not touch him, Cesare."

His son shrugged. "They must be stopped."

"I know. It will be too obvious. It will start a war between the papal states." Alexander drummed his fingers on his desk, lost in thought.

"He conspires with the French!" Cesare shouted, his dark eyes smoldering.

"They would love to start an inquiry, blame you for something...anything. I will never be able to protect you."

"I care not for the church, Papa. Let them take my robes. I'd rather soldier."

"Well, I care!" Alexander responded hotly, matching his son's anger. "You will be pope!"

"We must find another way." Cesare dug his knife into the table, carving a deep gouge.

"All eyes will be on you tonight." The pope shook his head. He brushed away the dagger, giving his son a filthy look.

Lucrezia's throaty laughter reached them, breaking their dark mood. Cesare smiled at his father. He looked at his sister, his face caressed by dark shadows. "She is no longer a child," he said craftily.

"No!" The pope, sensing his intent, pounded his fist on the table.

"Why? They'll never suspect her. She's barely fifteen. Sforza and Orsini are allies."

"Too dangerous."

"Not if we use this." Cesare reached into his pocket and pulled out a ruby ring. He held it up to his father, the red stone turning blood colored when the light from the window lit the fires inside its depths. Cesare slid his finger over the top of the gem, releasing a mechanism that revealed a hollow chamber perfect for a poison.

"No. I won't have her do that," Alexander said flatly.

"We all do what we must." Cesare arched a dark brow.

Alexander looked at his daughter. He made a rude noise. "She won't do it. She still has scruples." He shrugged. "She wouldn't even know how."

"She is a Borgia," Cesare said, his face close to his father. "She will learn." Cesare watched his younger sister, a dark gleam in his eyes. "She'll do it for me. She'll do it to belong. She has secrets too."

"What secrets?" Alexander demanded.

Cesare laughed, his face shadowed. "As if you don't know."

Alexander pulled at his bottom lip, deep in thought. "I don't like it."

"Neither do I, Papa, but it is her birthright as well. The family business, so to speak." Cesare laughed again.

"It's too dangerous."

"Our entire existence is surrounded by danger. She must learn to protect herself."

"You'll teach her?"

Cesare smiled, his face emerging from the shadows. "I plan to teach her many things."

"Lucrezia," Cesare called playfully. "Come, dearest. I am going to show you a powerful weapon."

Cesare took his sister's hand and led her into a private room. They sprawled across a sumptuous bed, the ring between them. "We are surrounded by enemies, sister," he began. "We have to use tools to protect ourselves and our interests."

"Politics," Lucrezia said importantly. "Papa has placed us all where we will yield the greatest influence. I still don't understand why he gave me to the Sforzas." Her face grew dark. "I hate him."

"Hate is a fool's weapon. It serves no purpose. I have a weapon that, when used the right way, will mow down our opponents and allow us to reign supreme."

He showed his sister the ring, explaining how it worked with poison.

"No, no, no. I don't want to do that!" Lucrezia flicked it to his side of the bed. "It's evil."

Cesare held the red gem up to her face. "You would prefer to let Papa suffer, or be thrown from power?" Cesare rose, circling the lavish room, his arms wide. "We will lose all this. You will be simply Lucrezia Sforza, a fat little housewife without the great papal influence to keep that idiot husband of yours in check."

Lucrezia shuddered delicately, the memories of her husband's brutish behavior fresh in her mind. "I will go to hell!" She rose to her knees, her hands clasped. "I am afraid of damnation." She whimpered.

Cesare laid his long frame on the bed, taking her hands within his large one, his voice soft. "Papa has said there is no such place as hell, little one. As long as you stay here with us, we will keep you safe." He placed the ring in her hand, then closed her fingers over it.

Lucrezia felt the cold stone against the palm of her hand. She held it close to her face, looking into the faceted depths, knowing she made her choice. She knew only of the hell with her husband and was willing to risk it all to stay away from him. Besides, she thought, her father said there was no hell, and he was the pope. He knew everything.

Chapter 14

Patrick slammed his beer onto the wet surface of the table.

Amanda jumped back, narrowly missing being splashed. "You idiot. Are you drunk?"

"Unlike some people, I only had one beer," Patrick said, sneering. "Look, if you're bored with me, go join them. Don't come running back when they stab you in the back."

"What are you talking about?" Amanda rubbed furiously with her napkin at a wet ring on the scarred wood.

"They're evil, those girls. I wouldn't associate with them." He shrugged indifferently. His cheeks were a fiery red, a telltale sign he was pissed.

"I'm not asking you to hang out with them. They're my friends. I've known them for years. You don't understand."

"Understand what? They're mean, Amanda. They crucified Tim Malloy when he broke up with Katherine. I don't like them."

"Her name is Kaitlyn. You don't know them," Amanda said through gritted teeth. "You're judging them."

"Ha!" He laughed. "I'm judging them? They are the most judgmental pieces of—"

"You're trying to make me choose between you!" she said hotly, panic welling in her chest. She couldn't choose. She needed them both—Patrick and her friends. They were her family; they had supported her through the whole custody thing when she told her father about Wayne. That had been an epic shit storm, and she had ended up at Children's Protective Services until her grandmother got there. Nana was sick already, and Amanda couldn't help but feel that her revelations had finished her off. Nana died a couple of years later, her heart broken by her daughter's selfish denials. Luckily, Danielle's parents had allowed Amanda to live with them so she could finish high school rather than move abroad with her father's new family. She didn't speak to her mom until Nana's funeral, and she found out that Natalie had left Albert over money. Some people took a little longer to make the right choice, she thought bitterly.

"So go!" Patrick yelled, bringing her back into the present.

"What is your problem?" She looked at him, resentment filling her chest. What right did he have to choose whom she would be friends with? True, he put up with her moodiness, the baggage from her youth, but she gave him a lot too. It wasn't as if she were a total troll. She loved him, for God's sake.

Patrick gazed into his drink darkly. Amanda made a disgusted noise and moved off her chair to walk to a group of laughing girls squeezed in a booth in the back of the room.

Danielle sat in the center, Kaitlyn practically on top of her. A new group of fawning acolytes had surrounded the two girls, totally absorbed, hanging on every word. Danielle's eyes narrowed suspiciously at Amanda, who stood watching the tableau. Amanda reached in and grabbed a french fry. Danielle slapped her hand, and the fry fell on the greasy tabletop. "Sit down if you are planning to eat our food," she ordered, her voice frosty. "Some people forget where they came from," she said caustically.

Amanda looked over her shoulder, watching Patrick trying to pretend he was ignoring her.

"He's an ass," Danielle said. "My parents practically raised you. Don't you forget that. You'd be speaking Chinese and eating fried rice if not for them."

"They live in Myanmar, not China," Amanda said, then added, "I'll never forget what I owe them, but Patrick's a great guy."

Danielle made a face. "I know he doesn't like me. I don't know what you've told him."

Amanda shook her head. She didn't have to tell him anything. Danielle had a mean mouth that loved to spin a rumor targeting weaker students, making her position of the most popular girl rock solid. She mowed down anyone who got in her way. She had easily been the coolest girl in high school, and she continued that role on campus. Amanda liked being associated with her. The loneness of her youth evaporated so that she finally had a place where she belonged, felt welcome. She even let Danielle push her into a communications major so they could study together. Amanda seriously considered a speech therapy career, but anytime she mentioned it, it sent Danielle into a tantrum. She looked at Danielle's pursed lips and frosty eyes. She glanced back at Patrick, seeing the hurt in his face. Her heart twisted in her chest. She liked Patrick, he was everything Danielle was not, and she was honest enough to admit she felt good when she was with him. She decided to defend Patrick. "That's not true. It's just…well…we are on a date, and he feels my place is with him."

"Blah, blah, blah." Danielle stopped her rambling with a cold stare. Amanda knew that look. Danielle could freeze out a person with a simple expression. Amanda had known that the minute she met her in high school. She had a healthy respect for Danielle's temper. Danielle was a greedy friend, demanding, spoiled, intolerant of anyone else's needs. Amanda looked at Danielle's perfect manicure, the hair tamed and styled as if she walked with a hairdresser attending her, the perfectly coordinated outfit, the five-hundred-dollar boots. Deep down inside, Amanda felt the seed of envy, the wish that she were Danielle. For a nanosecond, she had thought that living with Danielle and her family would rub off and she would have the patina of popularity as well. But it didn't happen. There was only one star in the household, and that star was Danielle. Danielle kept people at arm's distance and hanging on her every word, biddable and eager to please. She commanded and demanded with the strategy of a general. Amanda wanted to peel off the layers of her dumpy skin to try on Danielle's sleek version. She'd give anything to learn how to be confident enough to get what she wanted without regard for anyone's feelings. Danielle kept people at a distance because it worked for her—as opposed to plain old Amanda, whose childhood scars created impenetrable walls.

Amanda opened her mouth to make an excuse for Patrick again but thought better of it after seeing Danielle's hostile eyes. Kaitlyn shoved the platter of cheesy chili-covered fries so that it slid across the table.

"Such an ass," Kaitlyn repeated. The girls at the table—faceless, nameless beings—all nodded, their lollipop heads bobbing in unison. They looked like a collection of those bobblehead dolls that people had in the backs of their cars.

Amanda bristled. Danielle kicked out a stool in the guise of an invitation with her booted foot. Amanda looked at Patrick, who pointedly ignored her. She slid into the seat, her back bowed with defeat. She saw him shake his head with disgust; anger bubbled inside of her. Who did he think he was? She needed these girls. She had to survive. What if he left her at some point? Who would want her then? If she broke from them and something happened, she'd be alone—as she had been when she was a child. She would do whatever she had to do to keep in Danielle's good graces. Amanda was a survivor.

Danielle picked up a fry from the platter, scooping at the pile of yellow cheese that nothing in nature could ever have produced. The melted cheese cobwebbed as she pulled, her face mulishly indifferent. She offered it to Amanda.

Amanda accepted the limp fry and chewed it thoughtfully as she considered Danielle.

Danielle was tall, with pin-straight black hair and a perfect nose, her lips plumped with fillers. Her heavily lashed eyes gleamed with triumph in the low light of the bar. Patrick was a selfish beast for putting her in this position, Amanda thought. She needed them all. She'd fix it with him later, she thought with confidence.

"He's my boyfriend." She shrugged. "Patrick wants me to stay with him."

Kaitlyn gnawed the bones of a chicken wing. "He's too possessive." She talked with food in her mouth, bits of chicken spraying everywhere. "We invited him. He didn't even acknowledge Danielle."

A heinous crime. Everyone acknowledged Danielle. She was the gatekeeper to the best parties, the hot sorority. She made the difference whether a person was accepted or ignored.

Amanda looked at the bar where Patrick drank, his face set. He stared hard at her, then at the other girls. He didn't like them; he had made it clear. Amanda's lips tightened. They were like family, she had explained. Some things had to be endured.

Memories of the custody battle, Wayne's trial, and the ugliness that colored her life during the year she exposed her stepbrother pounded in her cortex. Filth from her mother's mouth still reverberated in her brain, the hurt lodging in her heart. Her father's hurried good-byes, her stepmother's cold responses, and finally Nana's broken heart filled every cell until she thought she would explode.

Anger swelled in her chest, and she directed it across the room at Patrick. Danielle had protected her when they relocated her. Embraced her, made room for her in her home, her clique. Her life would be hell if she lost them. Isolated, cold hell. She was right, he was wrong. It was as simple as that. She stomped over to him filled with indignant rage. The argument came back in full fury.

"The things that come out of their mouths, Amanda. I don't recognize you," Patrick said. He shook his head. "They are poison."

"You are jealous of my friendship with them!" Amanda yelled.

"No, I'm not," Patrick responded. "They're not nice. I don't..."

"You don't what?"

"I don't like who you are when you're with them."

"I don't know what you're talking about," Amanda said, but she knew that she did. She stormed off and slid into the booth with the girls again, knowing deep in her heart she was different when she was with them. She had to be, to fit in. It was attack or be attacked.

A shot of vodka appeared. Amanda knocked it back, her eyes glazing from the intensity of the liquor. Another was placed before her, and Amanda drank it, heedless of Patrick's bristling anger. He was talking to someone now, his back turned to her.

"He's too controlling," Kaitlyn said snidely.

"He can't dictate what you do," Danielle said loudly. "Or can he, Amanda?"

Amanda looked at Danielle, hearing the dangerous coldness in her voice. Her heart beat faster in her chest; her cheeks were numb. Sitting on the chair, she felt isolated, as if they had her in an interrogation. She heard laughter, their distorted faces breaking into leering grins, as if they were looking into a mirror in a fun house. She heard the poison leave her mouth, knowing the untruths were mean spirited.

"I don't care about him."

"I don't believe you," Danielle sneered.

Amanda's words were slurred. Another shot was placed at her elbow. "He's just okay, you know…nothing special." She held her thumb and forefinger together as if measuring something tiny. They all giggled and pointed to Patrick. Amanda felt sick as the lies left her mouth. She cupped her lips, feeling bile rise to the back of her throat. Patrick had to understand. He had to. She needed this group; she had to fit in, no matter what they represented. She drank again, looking at her boyfriend, saying more things she didn't understand. Soon, the whole bar was loud with snide chuckles. Patrick seemed to shrink before her eyes.

He rolled off the stool to stand before her. "Why are you doing this?"

Amanda laughed, sliding off the seat to fall in a heap on the floor. Everybody turned to the door.

From her spot on the floor, Amanda saw two feet in black boots planted wide apart. She heard music. *It was a waltz?* she thought groggily. *Black boots and a waltz?*

CHAPTER 15

Munich, 1939

A full orchestra was playing "Tales from the Vienna Woods." Waiters circulated drinks on tiny trays. Glittering gems sparkled under the multifaceted chandeliers. Women floated by in the arms of uniformed men, their long white gloves resting on strong arms.

There was the murmur of conversation, laughter, and the tinkling of crystal glasses clinking in excited toasts.

Amanda flew around the room, the satin of her pale dress belling out around her, the breeze from the french doors chilling her skin. Her hair was up, off her neck, and she felt graceful, tall, and elegant. Closing her eyes, she tilted her head, enjoying the music, the lightness of being held as if she were fine china.

Her feet grazed the floor; her partner was accomplished, used to leading, making her feel graceful. The arms held her, the swirling room spinning faster as her partner twirled her around the slick dance floor, her feet barely touching the polished wood.

He was going too fast, she wanted to tell him. She tightened her hand on his shoulder, and he laughed. He moved faster, the dizzying speed making everything spin, until the colors bled into one another so she could not tell where one face began and another ended.

Amanda's lungs tightened; she tried to suck in air; the pace of their dancing became faster and faster. She felt as though she were in a vacuum, her feet flying, a hand squeezing her waist. She needed to stop; she was going to be sick. Everything was wrong. She didn't belong. Nothing was making sense. This wasn't history. She wasn't even in class; something was wrong, terribly wrong. What was she doing out of her time, out of her skin? The one hand tightened its hold on her hip, becoming viselike, the other grasping her hand a steel claw.

She opened her eyes, a scream rising from her stomach, pushing away from the imprisoning hold. That face, that infamous face. The most hated man in history. The definition of evil. She was dead, in hell. What was she doing here, in his arms? How could this be happening? *Wake up!* she cried. *Wake up; let me wake from this nightmare!*

They continued to spin, and she felt the sleek fabric of her gown tangle on her legs, the tight embrace of...this was no dream. She recoiled in horror. Was she dead? Had she driven home drunk? Had she killed everybody and earned a place in hell? She was damned, and this was damnation. What else could this be? Amanda fisted her hands and pounded the khaki uniform. The nasty face smiled, his piercing blue eyes impaling her, the postage stamp of a mustache twitching.

"Noooo..." she wailed, squeezing her eyes tightly, trying desperately to avoid the horrible sight. What could she have done to deserve this?

The mad dancing continued. They spun around the room, the speed increasing, as if it were some demented dance. Hitler laughed, his hands holding her tightly. Lightheaded, Amanda felt the light receding. The possessive pressure eased, replaced by a lighter touch. A familiar voice brought her back. She opened her eyes and found Nick looking down at her.

He was holding her. He would take her home. He would get her out of here.

"I want to go home. Let me go," she pleaded, tears streaming down her heated face.

"Stop and think. This is about association," he said calmly, oddly detached. "Remember, memory is used to spark association."

"I don't want to do this anymore," she said, sobbing.

The spinning became less frenetic, they slowed, and Nick's voice intruded on her misery. "I'm sorry, but you don't have a choice."

Amanda opened her eyes. They danced in a widening circle. Nick became Hitler, Hitler became Nick. It went on in a sickening parody of a waltz.

"What am I doing here?" The music slowed, the frenzied turns wound down, and the room emptied but for the two of them.

"You're dancing," Nick whispered.

Amanda swallowed convulsively, gulping as if staving off nausea.

"I..." She thought for a minute. "Why am I dancing with the enemy?"

CHAPTER 16

The bar was loud with the sounds of the Friday-night crowd. Amanda looked up from the floor, seeing the hurt in Patrick's face. She glanced back at her friends, their faces elongated with laughter as if they were braying donkeys. They spewed poison at Patrick, skewering him with words.

Shame painted her face. Amanda crawled to her knees, pulling herself half onto the stool. In her state, she failed to register the panicked faces, their shouts sounded garbled in her ears. No one was listening to her. She had to make it right, but they wouldn't look at her.

"Stop," she called. She reached out for Patrick's hand. "I was lying. You have to stop." The words came out garbled, as if her mouth and brain were not cooperating.

The room filled with screams. Amanda faced her friends, imploring them to listen. It was wrong to do that to people, she explained. After what Wayne had done to her, she should know better, she thought, hating herself.

Nobody was listening. They were scrambling from their chairs; drinks were flying, the sharp retorts of explosions deafening her ears.

Amanda spun. The room turned into a kaleidoscope of colors, a crazy momentum of flying bodies and shattering glass surrounding her. Amanda tilted her heavy head, taking in the lone person standing in the doorway, his legs wide apart, an assault rifle in his hands.

Why was Nick shooting at them? she thought hazily.

Chapter 17

Amanda sat stunned at her desk, back in the lecture hall. She twisted to see Nick, his face emotionless, hers filled with revulsion.

"It was you!" She recoiled in horror. "It wasn't an accident."

The auditorium was deathly silent. "It was an accident. I didn't mean to…" Nick's face was lowered; his eyes wouldn't meet hers.

Amanda stood, her laptop falling unheeded to the floor. "You animal. You killed all those people." She smacked him then, feeling his body jerk with the impact. She pounded with her fists but felt nothing. Her mind shut down, her body pulled inward, and her heart cleaved in two. "How could you do that?" She looked around the room, tears making dual tracks down her white cheeks. "Why am I here?" She looked up to the professor. "Why am I here with *him*?"

Aristotle took a long drink from a bottle of water. He cleared his throat.

"Why am I here with *you*?" she sobbed.

"Well, which should we answer first? The boy?" Aristotle's bored gaze landed on Nick, who had shrunk into his seat. "He is not really here. He hasn't been all this time."

"That's impossible," Amanda shot back. "I see him. I heard him speak. I can touch him. He's as real as you are."

Aristotle steepled his fingers thoughtfully over his bulbous nose. "Is he, Amanda? So you finally believe everything you see. What did you think up until now? That you were in your school, taking a course you never registered for, with people you didn't know?" He pointed his fat, beringed finger at her. "This is your reality, not his."

"Reality is relative to the person living it."

"Hey, I'm no Einstein. If you wanted to talk about relativity, you should have signed up with him." He laughed, his great belly shaking. "I know." He turned his penetrating stare to Nick. "Let's give her a taste of *your* reality. What do you think of that, m'boy?"

Nick raised his face, his dark eyes pools of black misery, his pale skin white, the front of his T-shirt stained with red blood. He looked at Amanda, shaking his head. "Why do you have to question everything?" he whispered.

"That's the point!" Aristotle exclaimed, but Amanda heard him as if he were speaking from a distance. The room gelled; the faces of the other students became muddied, indistinct. Voices echoed, the sound distorting, changing into ear-splitting clanging that reverberated within her body. Amanda was hurled into the sky, flying straight up, the ground below her changing shape and colors, until it started coming at her in a dizzying rush. She landed with a crash, rolling on the lumpy, spongy ground. Rising on all fours, she felt her hands sink into the hot mud. She crawled on her knees, her hands stuck fast in the soil, as if her fingers had taken root. Her knees sank deep, the surface a viscous brown mass with a greenish miasma floating above it. The sulfurous smell caught in her throat, choking her. Struggling, she tried vainly to rise, but the tenacious mud pulled her closer into its odorous depths. Tears streamed down her face, and she wiped them with her shoulder. Craning her neck, she searched the dim surroundings for a familiar face. She heard a whining cry, a keening wail, bouncing through the soggy mess. Squinting, she searched. The gaseous clouds parted, and she saw a speck that moved closer, becoming clearer. Nick was buried to his neck, his head rolling spastically, his face caked with dried dirt, his hair matted with it. She saw him pause and then look up, his eyes round with fear. Looking into them, she screamed, closing her own eyes to the reflection she saw in his. Behind his skull a firestorm raged, with small, grotesque figures stoking the flames. They danced with indifference, soulless beings, pricking his consciousness back to life. Each time he forgot the pain, they prodded angrily, reminding him of his entire reason for being here, causing him to suffer forever.

Amanda wanted to cover her face, but her imprisoned hands prevented it. Falling forward, she landed near him, her face inches from his. His choked whispers seeped into her mind. "This is my reality. For eternity." He moved his lips, drool leaking on his chin. He looked at her piteously. "I'm sorry...I'm sorry..." he stuttered.

Amanda pulled with Herculean strength, her hand freeing from the thick mud. She rubbed it on her jeans, appalled by the odor.

Amanda backed away, realizing a multitude of voices were echoing those same words. She was surrounded. Gasping, she fell backward to sit in the mess, seeing a sea of faces, thousands of heads, their bodies buried in the muck, in various stages of decay but alive and suffering. She recognized them—famous people, the monsters of history who had inflicted pain and misery on their victims.

She scrambled to her feet and ran, her shins connecting with Stalin, Caligula, and Pol Pot. Wu Zetian, the Chinese empress famous for murdering thousands, including her own daughter, was next to Elizabeth Bathory, the countess who mutilated servant girls to bathe in her victims' blood. Josef Mengele, the Nazi doctor of death, was planted next to Heinrich Himmler, the accountant of death. And Maximilian Robespierre, architect of the bloodbath that was the French Revolution, cried out, his jaw hanging on a bit of flesh, his mouth working spasmodically, his face tormented. Faces she didn't know, murderers, Ted Bundy, John Wayne Gacy, Aileen Wuornos, people who acted without conscience—women and men—were now reduced to quivering masses of flesh, their faces gelatinous, their eyes filled with the same images that Nick saw. An army of pint-sized demons poked their brains, never letting them rest. They were all stuck in a private hell to suffer forever. The odor and stink were intolerable. Amanda gagged. She backed away, stepping on their faces, feeling them rest their heads wearily against her, looking for succor.

"No!" she yelled, raising her arms upward. She screamed again, her throat raw, her hands gripping her face with repugnance. She called out to Aristotle, and, in a blink, she was seated, the sounds and smells gone. It was dead quiet.

"No time for that now." Aristotle's voice was the only thing she heard now.

Amanda looked up to find his face searching hers. She put her head into her hands, sobbing. "I don't want to die. I don't want to die."

"Tsk...who said anything about dying?" Aristotle said impatiently.

The room was empty. It was just the two of them. Her broken sobs filled the lecture hall.

"So you see, sleep is essential when the body's senses have been overstimulated. All your critical activities, such as sensing, thinking, and using your memory, do not function in the same way as when you are awake. While you typically can't sense things while you are asleep, you can have a sensory experience." The teacher paused, sighing gustily. "Are you getting all this, Amanda?" he asked impatiently.

Amanda shuddered convulsively. "You mean I'm not dead?" she asked brokenly.

"The greatest mind in the universe, and all she cares about is whether she's alive or dead." He threw his hands into the air. "No, Amanda, you are not quite dead, but…" He looked her full in the face. "You are not quite alive, either."

"What does that mean?" she wailed. "And what happened to Patrick and Danielle and all the others? Why did you make me sit through those boring lectures?"

Aristotle studied her thoughtfully. "As I was saying—"

Amanda groaned, letting her head fall forward, tears painting her hot face, her chest heaving as the old man droned on.

"We encounter stimuli all day, and that leaves lasting impressions in our consciousness. When we sleep, those impressions become noticeable because we are not distracted by the workings of life. When we sleep, the lines of judgment between fact and fantasy become blurred, which leads to the amazing inventions of imagination. In other words, our fancy takes flight!" he crowed. "You see, when the images become dreams, and since common sense is technically turned off, if you will, reality changes. And the dreams do not actually resemble the actual experience…"

The room faded, and the constant beep of machinery entered her consciousness. Amanda floated, warring whether to stay or go. Go where? Her thoughts scattered. Her chest tightened with the feeling she was being watched; the flapping black coat teased her peripheral vision. Her hands fisted impotently, but she felt trapped, tied down. Everything was gone but a white mist and kind hands that stroked her head.

Amanda calmed her brain, taking stock of her senses. The hands caressed her skin. Soft words were spoken. They were garbled yet comforting, the voice familiar. She smelled the comforting fragrance of nutmeg and cinnamon. Her mouth watered for rice pudding; her stomach growled. She inhaled like a puppy searching for the smells that meant home or someone she loved. In her mind's eye, she reached out for the scent. She knew that song, recognized the voice. Tears of relief prickled her eyelids. "Nana," she sighed. Her mouth moved in time to the song.

"Have a taste of sparkly star, and drink a sip of moon, and when you feel as though you have gone far, then sail into your room." Her grandmother's voice shimmied and swirled into her mind, the words of the song inflating her heart with love.

"Nana," she repeated, happiness flooding her.

Nana sang again. Amanda cracked her eyes open, the light blinding her at first. She eased her eyes open wider, seeing the luminous face watching her. She tried to reach out but couldn't. Her grandmother embraced her, coating her with peace.

"You have to go back now, Manda. It's not your time."

Amanda swallowed thickly, giving reality to what scared her most. "But I think I'm dead."

"No." Her grandmother shook her head. "You'll heal. You always do. If you learn, you'll heal."

"Learn?"

Her grandmother smiled. "We all learn. Even the Joan of Arcs and Lucrezia Borgias of this world."

"I don't understand."

"Time and history are a continuum. A constant flow of energy that works symbiotically together."

"English, please," Amanda said imploringly.

"In some cases, we learn from the mistakes of others. In other cases, we use the experiences of people to spark a memory for us to learn about ourselves."

Amanda rolled her eyes. "Ugh. Now you sound like Aristotle."

"Gave you a hard time, did he?"

"I still can't make sense of anything."

"It's all very simple. Each person comes here, to this place, to learn lessons. Their lessons join the communal consciousness for us all, so we can all grow from other people's observations."

"But all that stuff about the wars, names, and dates. That's real history, not what I experienced."

"No, dear," Nana said patiently. "Those are facts, mere incidentals. Don't you understand? History is about the people, the flesh-and-blood people and their reactions to the challenges of life. They set the precedent for us to learn how to go on. You understand?" She raised a white eyebrow.

"So we don't repeat the same mistakes."

Amanda sat up in her bed, her shackles gone, her hands free. She looked around the hazy room. She was in a hospital, the entire back wall filled with monitors. The halls echoed with the soft footsteps of nurses.

"So, why Joan of Arc? I had nothing in common with her. I didn't learn anything from her."

"A means to an end. She was there for you to first recall who you are, and then to define you as a person. The heat of her sacrifice lit the spark for you to remember your own past so you could move forward."

"Wayne and my mother did not mold me in any way!" Amanda said hotly.

Her grandmother sat on the edge of the bed and rested her hand on Amanda's folded ones. "It made you sensitive but overly protective. Aware of your surroundings, distrustful."

"So...okay. Lucrezia?"

"Lucrezia was a gentle reminder from me." Nana inclined her head. "Don't let life poison you. Lucrezia used poison to get what she wanted. I didn't want you to repeat the error. That was a life lesson."

"And Nick?" Amanda shuddered. "Hitler?"

"The tools to get you there."

Amanda gasped. "Patrick! My friends?"

"I think now you remember what happened to them."

Two shadows crisscrossed the room, filling it with an intense coldness. Amanda shivered, feeling afraid. She gasped and moved closer to the energy of her grandmother. She looked around for the snap of the black coat, knowing it was close. She felt the cold chill of him breathing down her neck. The two shadows moved restlessly, the outline of a black hat nearby, the shape of a man in the doorway in the opposite direction. Two opposing forces warring for possession of the room.

"I'm afraid." Amanda shivered.

Nana stood, moving to the right side of the room. She flapped her arms. "Go away. She's not ready," she called out to the dark presence. She turned back to Amanda "I tell you, that Death." She shook her head. "He's a greedy one."

Amanda reached for her grandmother. "If that was Death, why did Nick always keep him at bay?"

"We go back to Aristotle again, my dear. Nick was there to make you remember. He was never truly with you. He was the lasting impression created by your mind so you could sort out what had happened."

"So it was all a dream?" Amanda asked incredulously.

Her grandmother laughed. "Row, row, row your boat, Amanda. You remember the nursery rhyme. What is life but a dream?"

"Since when did you become so philosophical?" Amanda asked tartly.

"Aristotle's not the only guy giving classes!"

The dark specter moved deeper into the room, and Amanda backed away from it.

Nana turned back to Amanda. "You're not ready, are you? You want to stay?"

Amanda looked at the shadow on the left. It solidified, tall with broad shoulders, a cap of blond hair, that square chin that showed determination rather than stubbornness. Amanda's heart lifted, and her soul rejoiced. Patrick moved into the room. He stared at the bed, his light eyes hollow, a bandage on his hand. He sat gingerly next to her, placing his warm hand over her own. She felt the crinkly cellophane of a Lifesaver candy placed securely in her palm. He squeezed her hand tenderly, tears leaking from his eyes.

Amanda felt her lids droop, and her mind drifted back. She saw the bar and her friends surrounding her. She faced a spotted mirror, the surface reflecting the entrance. Patrick stood next to her, angrily asking what she was doing. The leering laughter of her companions gave it a carnival atmosphere. She was drunk, sliding off her chair to land in a heap on the greasy floor. The club was noisy with laughter and music. She noticed a man entering. She saw his dusty boots and the open biker jacket he wore over a white tee. She looked up to see his dark eyes and the beginning of a beard on his narrow face. His eyes were shiny, his cheeks taut with suppressed anger. The muzzle of a gun rested against his black-clad leg. The man pointed the weapon in Patrick's direction.

Amanda rose clumsily, her arm brushing her drink off the table to shatter on the floor, her only thoughts for Patrick. Leaping high, she flew toward him as a hail of bullets spit across the room. She saw people fall, blood spurting; the floor was slick with it. Danielle landed, her shoulder in a splatter of blood and bone, and Kaitlyn collapsed next to her in a dead faint. Screams erupted, time slowed, and movements became turgid, as if they were underwater. She spun, impacted, the bullet punching her back. She remembered surprise at the lack of pain, only the horror of Patrick's face when she threw herself in front of him, preventing his death but creating her own.

She heard Patrick scream and felt the warmth of his body over her, and then the sounds receded to thick silence.

Her grandmother patiently watched the play of emotions on her face.

"I want to stay," she said simply.

"Then learn from the universal consciousness. Don't repeat their mistakes."

"I'll miss you, Nana," she said, holding out her arms.

"I'll always be nearby. See you in sixty or seventy years." A cool kiss touched her brow. Amanda sighed deeply, opened her eyes, and rejoined the living.

Author's Note

I have long believed that we do indeed go to a special place when we die to meet up with friends and family and reexamine our lives. I have always wondered what happens to all those great minds when they leave the corporeal plane. Could you imagine being able to reconnect and learn from the finest intellects created?

So Amanda finds herself in the exalted company of Aristotle, Alexander the Great's teacher, while in her drug-induced coma. Why not? He did write about dreams in three treatises: *On Sleep and Dreams*, *On Sleeping and Waking*, and finally, *On Divination through Sleep*. He believed that our dreams are the products of experiences we have while awake, and because common sense is essentially "turned off" when we sleep, our minds can create those crazy but realistic flights of fantasy.

While Amanda is in that in-between place, not quite dead but barely alive, her tortured psyche needs to sort out the horror that has put her there. So, utilizing Aristotle's theory, I used history as the conduit for her to both discover her own past and decide her fate.

I do not believe in hell as I describe it. However, I think troubled souls do end up in a special place where they must reexamine their mistakes and eventually atone for them.

So the question remains: Did Amanda truly dream it all, or did history lend a helping hand?

Made in the USA
Charleston, SC
19 December 2015